LOST *and* FOUND

To Louise

much happiness

Lucinda Race

Lucinda Race

To my dear husband, Rick
Life with you is better than a dream

To the LR posse
Shirley, for encouraging me to start with page one
Cheryl, for reading each revision
Megan and Emily, for listening to all the early stories
Kathy, for being patient with a newbie

To Sabrina
Your illustrations bring Loudon to life

To Ann
Because of you, Cari has her home

A special thanks to the team at
Berkshire Media Marketing

*You know you're in love when you can't fall asleep
because reality is better than your dreams.*
— Dr. Seuss

Contents

Chapter One

CARI PEERED THROUGH THE RAIN-COVERED WINDSHIELD. The wipers thudded as they slapped from side to side, and her car's headlights barely illuminated the road ahead. The humidity hung heavy with the threat of bad weather. A nasty storm had barreled through and deluged the area just as she had closed the shop. She should have taken the weatherman seriously when he predicted severe weather.

Cari's stomach tightened with each rumble of thunder. Suddenly, a huge bolt of lightning crashed just beyond the tree line. She had never been a fan of storms and it seemed they'd grown more severe lately. Maybe there was something to global warming.

Her street was just ahead and relief coursed through her. The road was inundated with water. Lightly tapping the brakes she turned left onto Maple Street just as it was plunged into darkness. Anxious to get home safely she drove slowly down the street, avoiding the debris and dodging the trees as they bent low, kissing the ground. The bright headlights swept over the driveway as she pulled up to the garage door. She waited impatiently for it to open wide enough to get the car stowed inside.

Cari dashed to the back door, firmly slamming it behind her. Leaning against it, she took deep breaths to steady her pulse as the hair on her arms stood on end. A thunderous crack rang out immediately followed by a large bolt of lightning that illuminated the room. Oh no, she thought, realizing that what had been struck was very close to where she stood. She felt the house shudder and then—deafening silence.

Cari pulled herself together and crossed the room. As she peered out the kitchen window, she was shocked to discover that the large pine tree, which had dominated the back yard, was now resting on the roof of her house. It had split down the middle and hefty chunks of trunk and branches covered the ground. The sunroom was in shambles, and shards of glass and wood splinters littered the floor. Stunned, she stared at the carnage as the sun broke through the dark heavy cloud cover.

"For crying out loud, Ben, look at what your stupid tree did! I told you not to plant it so close to the house. They grow about a foot per year, so that means your tiny tree grew into a twenty-five-foot monster," Cari screamed.

Cari flung open the back door and stepped into heavy pine-scented air. For a brief second she inhaled deeply, savoring the cool, fresh air the storm had left after washing away the oppressive heat.

She gingerly picked her way through the branches that peppered the lawn.

"Ben, what are we going to do? One side of the house is devastated," she cried. "I'll call Shane. This mess needs heavy equipment. I'm sure he'll bring the guys over to clean it up."

Ray glanced out the dining room window curious if he could see what got struck by lightning. To his surprise, his neighbor was standing in front of a large tree, which had become a part of her house. Her long slender hands flew through the air as she carried on an animated conversation with the tree. Ray pulled on his work boots and headed over to see what he could do to help.

Cari was intently surveying the damage and muttering to herself as Ray came over. He could tell she hadn't heard him, so he cleared his throat and ventured, "Ah, Cari, are you okay?"

Cari turned, relieved to see Ray, standing three feet away from her. At six-foot-three, he towered over her. She jammed her hands into her front jean pockets, feeling foolish for having been caught talking to herself.

Gesturing to the pieces of tree that lay before them, she said, "Well, I guess my day ended with a bang. This little seedling Ben planted decided it didn't want to be in the rain, so it came inside the house. Unfortunately for me it didn't come in as firewood," she said ruefully. "A couple of years ago Shane wanted to cut it down. But no, I had to be stubborn. I told him there was no reason to cut it down because it was healthy. In hindsight, I guess I should have listened to reason. I just didn't want anything changed in the yard."

"Hey, don't beat yourself up. No one knows when or where lightning will strike—it just happens. Have you called your son yet? I can stick around and give him a hand. We should drape a tarp over the hole in the roof before it gets dark."

"That's so nice of you to offer your help but I don't have a tarp. This is so frustrating! I can't believe this happened."

"I've got one in my shop that you can borrow until you figure something out. I'll run over, get it, and be right back." He jogged across the connecting yards.

Pulling her cell phone out of her back pocket, she pushed a number on speed dial.

Trying her best to sound casual, she said, "Hi, Shane, it's Mom. Wasn't that a doozy of a storm?"

"Hey, Mom, everything is fine here at the lake, but it was pretty bad!"

"That's an understatement. Any chance you can swing by?" Cari paused. "Before you say 'I told you so,' I need to tell you something."

"Okay, what's going on?" Shane knew why she was calling. It was just a matter of time before a storm brought down the pine tree.

"Remember that large pine tree in the backyard, the one you told me needed to be cut down? Well, it got struck by lightning, split down the center, and fell on the house."

"You're kidding. The tree got hit?" He let out a low whistle. "How bad is it? Should I call Don, too?"

"No, don't bother your brother-in-law tonight. Ray was here and just left to get a tarp to cover up the hole. But you're going to need a ladder," Cari stated flatly while staring at the roofline.

"Alright. Hang tight and I'll see you soon." Shane abruptly disconnected.

Cari went into the kitchen to grab cold drinks. She and Ray might as well be social while waiting for Shane. Cari was fortunate to have a good neighbor in Ray. He was always willing to lend a hand when needed. She dealt with the loneliness most days, but at this second, she missed her husband.

Her eyes followed Ray as he made his way back to the deck. He was all male, and the proverbial tall, dark, and handsome variety. His features were strong and sharp without being harsh, enhanced by dark hair that swept down over cool blue eyes that a girl could easily drown in. Why he didn't have a girlfriend was beyond her. Trotting next to Ray was Gifford, a fifty-pound ball of fur whose tail was always wagging. Gifford turned up on Ray's back steps one day and Ray adopted him then and there. Now the two were inseparable.

Ray carried a huge, blue plastic bundle in his arms. "Here's the tarp," he said while Gifford dropped to the ground and promptly started a gentle dog snore, exhausted from the long walk across the yard.

"That's overkill, isn't it?" Cari joked, as she handed him a cold beer.

"You're kidding right? Did you see the gaping hole in your roof? I'm worried it won't be big enough!"

"You could be a little more optimistic, Ray." Cari was saddened to see the devastation of her beloved home.

Cari watched Ray take a slug of his beer. She sipped her own and wished Shane would hurry up. Thankfully, it wasn't long before his truck appeared around the side of the garage, coming to an abrupt stop on the lawn. Climbing out, he took in the full extent of what had happened. Shane crossed the lawn, eating up the distance between them. He was the spitting image of his father—long, lean, and muscular—but had inherited his mother's black hair, green eyes, and a quick, easy smile. By twenty-five he'd established a reputation in the community for his hard work and honesty with his landscaping business. He worked side-by-side with his crew at every site, getting the job done safely and on time. Cari was proud of her only son.

Shane extended his hand, "Good to see you, Ray. Did you see the tree come down or just hear Mom yelling at it?" The men chuckled.

"This isn't funny, and I don't appreciate that you two are laughing at my expense!" Cari burst out at them.

"Mom, I'll take the blame on this. I should have insisted you take the tree down before now. I knew we were on borrowed time. I know you and Dad planted it to commemorate buying the house, but now it's going to take some serious work to get everything cleaned up and the house fixed." Shane could tell his comment touched a nerve so he softened his approach. "Let's go see how bad it is and then get the tarp slung over the hole as best we can. Tomorrow we can get things moving."

Shane and Ray checked out the mess from all angles and discussed the best way to get the tree off the house without additional damage to what was left of the structure. Cari trailed along behind the guys, wishing she had listened to her son years ago.

Cari couldn't help but stare at the tree branches jutting out from the glassless windows.

"Ben," she hissed, "do you see what a mess this is? Can you imagine how much money it will take to fix it?"

Fuming, Cari stormed into the house and slammed the back door harder than she had intended. She grabbed a beer for Shane and went back outside. It gave her a couple of minutes to pull herself together. The guys walked toward Cari, with Gifford at their heels.

Taking a deep breath, she prepared herself for the bad news. "Any possibility we can get the tree off of the house tonight? I hate the idea of the house being exposed to whatever little critters and wiggly things that might find their way inside."

"Mom, I'm sorry. The best we can do is draping the tarp over the hole. I can have my crew here bright and early tomorrow. You should get pictures before the sun sets for the insurance company. Tomorrow morning the guys will get the tree off the house and clean up the debris. Don and I will come back to get the logs cut up for firewood. It's not safe to do anything more tonight."

Frustrated with the news, Cari shrugged her shoulders. Shane retrieved the extension ladder from his truck, setting it against a solid wall of the house. Ray handed up a side of the tarp and together they pulled it over the gaping hole. Shane stole a glance at his mom as they worked. Patience wasn't one of his mother's virtues.

Ray couldn't take his eyes off Cari. Despite the current situation, her beauty struck him. Shining emerald green eyes were fringed with long, dark lashes. Auburn streaks highlighted in ebony hair, which framed her delicate features. She could stop a man in his tracks, he thought.

Ray wanted to help. "Cari, I can give you names of a few good contractors. The insurance company will request several estimates. If you'd like, I can give you an estimate for repairs, it will give you something to compare with the other estimates. I'm happy to explain any terms you're not familiar with. Just give me a shout."

Ray's gentle tone soothed her raw emotions. "I guess I don't have a lot of choices at the moment. I'll have to be patient until everything is cleaned up. Ray, thank you for being so understanding. You've been so nice about all this, and I really do appreciate your help."

"I'm going to head home, Mom. Try not to worry about everything tonight and get some sleep. Tomorrow is another day." Shane hugged his mom.

"And Cari, if you're all set I'm going to take off, too. Unless you need something, and then I'm happy to hang around for a while longer." Ray wasn't in a rush to leave, but he didn't have a good excuse to stay.

"No, I'm all set. Thanks again, Ray, for everything. You were a big help tonight. I'll see you tomorrow at the shop? Breakfast is on me, okay? After all, it's the least I can do." Cari gave him a lopsided smile.

"You don't need to buy me breakfast, but thanks. I never miss the most important meal of the day," he teased. "Good night, Cari." With a jaunty wave, he went home.

Alone and with a heavy heart, Cari slowly walked into her house. She found herself inexplicably drawn to what was left of the sunroom. Standing on the threshold, she peered into the gloomy darkness left by the long shadows cast by the tree. Scanning, she could see her piano on the other side of the room. Unsure of its condition, she picked a path over the debris and to her delight discovered the old baby grand and her treasured family photos sitting atop it were in pristine condition. The cushions on her overstuffed chair and ottoman were littered with pine needles but otherwise untouched. Ben had given her the set when Ellie, her youngest daughter, was born. She was amazed at the total destruction on one side while the other remained untouched.

The ivory keys called to her, willing her fingers to lovingly caress them from rich low bass tones to sweet high notes. She studied the photos on display, frozen moments of a full and happy life: a wedding photo with Ben and one of their newborn twins, Kate and Shane. She reached out to study a picture of the twins tucked in a chair and proudly cradling Ellie the day she came home from the hospital. She could still hear Kate tell her that baby Eleanor looked like a pixie, with wispy blond hair and crystal blue eyes, long eyelashes, and dimples. She had begged Cari to rename her Pixie Dust. She and Ben had laughed it off, but the nickname stuck.

Cari set the picture down. She continued her journey down memory lane until her eyes came to rest on a framed photo. She, Ben, and the kids were grinning despite the cold, gathered around a freshly cut Christmas tree. It turned out to be their last trip to the tree farm as a family. The smiling faces in the photo weren't prepared for the heartache to come the following spring, when five became four.

Cari dropped to the bench in front of the keys. Unaware of what she would play, her fingers found a melody. Raw emotions bubbled up from the depths of her soul. Slow and thick with emotion, music began to drift to the heavens.

Soft notes wafted over to Ray sitting in the dark on his patio. The melody tugged at his heart. In his mind's eye, he could see tears sliding unnoticed down Cari's cheeks. There had been countless nights when she played for an unseen audience.

As Ray listened, tonight wasn't any different. Cari poured her heart and soul into each note, emotions floating on the summer night's breeze. As the night wore on, she migrated to soft romantic jazz. Working through pain that had nothing to do with wood and plaster, Cari was releasing a part of her past that had been taken from her forever.

Cari played music late into the night as a feeling of peace enveloped her. She glanced up through what used to be the roof. Pinpoints of light dotted the heavens. Hugging her arms tight around her against the chilly night air, she made a wish on the stars. Turning on the bench, she took one last look around the room. Countless moments—wonderful, bittersweet, and heart-breaking—had taken place within these walls. Cari knew it was time for changes that went beyond paint on the walls and new curtains. Rebuilding would be the first step in making a fresh start but there would need to be significant changes. Cari decided to speak with Ray tomorrow. She wondered what could be possible without changing the footprint of the house. Exhaustion invaded her bones. New ideas would have to wait until tomorrow. Without a backward glance she left the room and crawled up the stairs. Sliding between the cool sheets, emotionally drained, she fell into a dreamless sleep.

Chapter Two

CARI AWOKE TO THE SOUND OF CHAINSAWS BUZZING in the backyard. She pulled on a pair of jeans and a lavender T-shirt before wandering barefoot into the kitchen. She glanced out the back window but didn't see Shane in the hubbub. With a cup of her secret blend in hand she sat down to enjoy a few minutes of relative calm before heading down to her shop, What's Perkin'. Kate would have muffins and scones baking, filling the shop with tantalizing aromas that made them irresistible to customers.

Cari smiled to herself thinking about how life had changed over the last few years. Kate had become an unexpected asset to the business. Initially, she moved back to Loudon after college. She planned to save some money and move to Boston, but Donovan Price, now her husband, followed Kate to Loudon.

Kate had graduated top of her class from Johnson and Wales University with a degree in culinary arts, which allowed Cari to relinquish full control of the kitchen to her creative daughter. She was happy at What's Perkin' and currently developing an expansion plan. Kate had always been the quiet child, and, at times after Ben died, it seemed she had been short-changed. Shane grew up overnight and assumed his father's role as man of the family. Ellie was so young she needed extra attention from Cari. Kate had quietly gone about her young life, helping her mother when needed and retreating into books every other spare moment.

Cari drifted back to the last morning she kissed Ben good-bye. It was like any other day except he never came home. The doctor assured Cari he hadn't suffered when the aneurysm struck him down. It was quick, and in all likelihood, he never knew what was going to happen. But she and the kids felt the pain.

Cari had stumbled through the first few days in a haze. Thank heavens for the kids. They were her anchor and reason for getting out of bed in the morning. Throughout their marriage, Ben had been her rock and best friend. With Ben by her side, Cari felt she could conquer anything. After several months had passed, she started to feel that Ben was still with her. She began talking to him. Her parents, Dave and Susan, knew about the conversations and weren't concerned. It helped Cari deal with her grief.

When the kids were small, Cari dreamed of opening a bakery. For years, Ben encouraged her to take the leap, and together they developed a solid business plan. Ben believed Loudon needed a place where locals and weekenders could get a good cup of coffee or tea and enjoy homemade baked goods. It would be the perfect business for Cari. But she had one excuse after another and didn't make the time to open a shop until the bottom dropped out of her world. After the overwhelming grief began to subside, Cari had to show the kids that life would go on and, together they'd get through the tragedy.

More than a year passed before What's Perkin' opened. It had been a difficult decision but Cari needed to have something to occupy her time while the children were at school. In the early days, people stopped in to lend their support, but after a while the food became the focus and most of the townies became regulars. Cari catered to the local community, running specials for the workweek and holidays. As the years flew by, the business thrived, and the McKenna family held events to support the local soup kitchen and food pantry. It was important to Cari that she continued to repay the kindness her family was given during their darkest days.

Silence jarred Cari back to the present. Shane's guys had finished. Glancing at the kitchen clock, she realized Kate had been single-handedly taking care of the shop for more than an hour and would need help. Cari grabbed her shoulder bag and hustled to the garage for the short two-mile drive to her home away from home.

The bell on the door rang causing Kate to pause and look up, hoping this time it was her mother. Usually Cari was the first one to arrive in the morning. Kate received a call from Shane the night before to update her and Don about the lightning strike. It was understandable that her mom was running late. Kate was worried about Cari's state of mind. Nothing had changed at the house since her dad passed away years ago.

Kate was waiting behind the long wooden counter when the door opened. A smile slid over her face to greet Cari. Relief lit up her blazing green eyes, Kate was the female version of Shane—graceful, slender, and tall. Her thick ebony hair flecked with auburn and golden highlights hung in a braid down her back.

"Hi, I was beginning to think I would be flying solo today. Thank goodness it's been slow," Kate teased.

"Hi, sweetheart." Cari hastily pulled the door shut behind her to keep the cool air inside. "I'm sorry I'm late. I got distracted. Shane's guys made short work of the cleanup. I'm sure the neighbors weren't happy they started so early. But it's done. Later today, Ray's going to stop at the house and give me an estimate."

Kate couldn't help laughing out loud. "Mom, are you going to take a breath this morning or talk nonstop? How about I fix you something to eat. I am assuming you had coffee but skipped breakfast."

"Hmmm, an egg sandwich would be tasty with cheese and ketchup?" Suddenly ravenous Cari's mouth watered. Dinner never crossed her mind in the craziness of the previous evening.

Kate stepped into the spacious, well-designed kitchen. The oversize center work area had easy access to essential equipment stored below, a commercial range, baking ovens lining one end, and cooling racks standing next to them. A large walk-in refrigerator was behind the center island, sinks and the dishwashing area was to the left. A wall was open down to counter height, separating the kitchen from the shop.

Baked items were cooling on the counter, ready for the display case. Her mom had taken seriously the construction of the kitchen and hired Ray to customize the workspace. The kitchen had taken months to complete and it was worth the effort—the workflow was flawless.

While she waited, Cari tidied up the front counter. She was restocking the display cases with fresh muffins, biscuits, and brewed a fresh pot of coffee as the door opened. Cari greeted Ray with a sunny smile.

"Hello there, neighbor! I hope the chainsaws didn't bother you this morning. Shane's guys got to my house pretty early."

"Nope, I didn't hear anything, and even if I had I am always up early."

Laughing, he said, "I have to make hay while the sun shines. Before we know it the days will grow short and we'll be indoors, trying to stay warm and dreaming of spring."

Conversation between the old friends flowed effortlessly.

For Ray the high point of every day was stopping in to visit with Cari before he started his day. This morning, in her jeans and ponytail, she looked more like a teenager than the mother of three grown children. Ray swore she got prettier all the time.

"What can I get for you? Coffee and a freshly baked muffin? They're straight from the oven." Cari gestured to the plate in the front case.

"A blueberry muffin, please. No, make that two, they smell amazing. Can you throw in a couple extra pats of butter in the bag? And a large coffee with cream and sugar. That should hold me temporarily."

Cari chuckled as she filled a bag. "Mr. Davis, you're going to turn blue with as many as you've eaten this summer. You order the same thing every day. Maybe tomorrow you can try something else, apple turnover or coffee cake muffins?" Cari teased.

Ray broke out in a belly laugh. "Well, it's your fault. You make them every day so how can I resist, they're my favorite. But maybe I'll change my order, if Kate takes requests from humble carpenters. How about blueberry scones? I'm sure she's made them before but I'm happy to be the official taste tester."

Ray wouldn't admit his weakness wasn't blueberry muffins.

"I'll check with Kate and see what we can do about adding some variety into your routine. We're always happy to take care of our loyal customers."

"I'll give you a call after I swing by your house and assess the damage. Then I should be able to give you a realistic estimate and a list of contractors for you to call for comparisons."

Cari nodded. "Alright, I should be home about five. Why don't you stop by and you can help me figure out what I need to do next?"

He started to agree but before he could get a word in, she kept on talking.

"You're a great carpenter and in high demand. I won't pull you away from the new kitchen remodel you got over in Litchfield, or any other jobs you have lined up, just to help me out," she said firmly.

"Cari, we're friends, and if I have time to help then I will. I'll be over later." Ray was out the door before she could protest. She heard him whistling as the door slammed behind him.

Jamming her hands in the pockets of her apron, she wondered what had just happened. The hole in her house wasn't his problem but he was determined to help. The last thing she wanted was to burden to anyone, especially Ray.

Cari's thoughts wandered back to when she met Ben. One winter day he was crossing the college campus and saw Cari from a distance. Her laughter reached him, and he had to meet her. It didn't take long for the couple to fall in love. When their relationship evolved to marriage, it didn't take much to convince Ben that Loudon was the best place to raise a family. He would have followed her anywhere. Small-town life had been good to them. They had been deliriously happy for thirteen short years.

Leaning on the counter while absently staring out the door, Cari caught a glimpse of her best friend, Grace Bell. She was making a beeline to her shop. Grace was tall and thin with bouncy blond curls and huge, soft brown eyes. The two girls had met while working in a diner and instantly had become best friends. Cari wondered how she would have gotten through the tough days without Grace and her husband, Charlie.

"Hey Cari, did I just see Ray leaving? He was looking pretty hot this morning. I think he's here more than I am!" Grace snickered as a surprised look flitted across Cari's face.

"He lives alone and I don't think he can cook to save his soul. You always said I made the best coffee, so it makes sense! Besides, just because you're my oldest friend doesn't give you the right to irritate me this morning!"

Grace couldn't contain herself any longer. "GF, for a girl who is so tuned into the universe sometimes you can be clueless."

Before Cari got the chance to ask what Grace meant several high school students came into the shop.

While Cari was occupied, Grace filled her travel mug at the self-service area, dropped a couple of bucks on the counter, and waved good-bye. Cari gave a quick wave knowing Grace would be back later. Kate had kept busy in the kitchen but could hear the conversations between her mother and the customers. She hadn't been able to figure out what was going on with her mother and Ray, but she had some ideas. Kate thought it was time she and Grace compared notes.

Kate thought about the recent conversation she had had with Shane and Ellie. They were all worried she spent too much time alone. Every night and weekend she puttered around the house and garden. They wanted Cari to have a full life, just as she had encouraged them to have.

Shane and Kate lived within a few miles of Cari, but with enough distance to have independence. Ellie was finishing her junior year in college. She was planning on early graduation and had been taking extra classes each semester. Technically, she lived at home but rarely spent much time there, using it as a pit stop for clean clothes and a quick meal. She crashed with friends at school to maximize her study time. When she had free time, Ellie helped out at the shop. She loved the bakery but her passion was for art and photography. Kate was confident Ellie would figure out how to combine what she loved into a career. Maybe the tree falling on the house was the best thing that could have happened for all of them, she mused. It had certainly shaken things up with her mother and Ray. If things went the way Kate hoped, Ray and Cari would be spending time a lot more time together.

Kate walked through the swinging doors. "Mom, ready to eat?" She grabbed two mugs of coffee and sat down at a small wooden bistro table. "It's quiet for the moment so you don't need to inhale your breakfast. If we get any customers I'll take care of them. You relax and enjoy."

Protesting, Cari said, "You have too much to do in the kitchen to take care of the front, too."

"I have plenty of time before I need to start baking the next batch of . . ."

Cari interrupted her. "That reminds me, Kate. This morning I was teasing Ray about his choice of breakfast foods. He put in a request for blueberry scones. But I was thinking, in addition to scones, do you think we could whip up something different, and maybe call it something special in honor of him? After all, he's been a loyal customer since we opened the shop. Maybe a twist on an old favorite?"

"Sure, I'll make scones and whip up something tasty," she replied and then casually asked, "Did I hear him say he's going to the house later?"

"Yes, he is going to check the structure. He's also offered to help me find a good contractor. I had wanted some new shelves so I'm thinking I can add them to the new plans. I don't think they will be much of an issue," she said ruefully.

Cari munched on her breakfast sandwich, noticing half of the plate was sliced fruit. Her daughter thought she was very clever, slipping fruits and vegetables onto a plate whenever she could. Grateful for a caring daughter, she ate every delicious bite.

Kate loved What's Perkin' as much as her mom did. She was proud of the menu and how the business flourished over the past fifteen years. During the last year, Kate added a small selection of specialty items, including a tiered cupcake display that tasted as good as it looked and had been used as a wedding cake. Cupcakes were becoming the most requested item, and Kate provided an abundance of unique combinations of cake flavors and fillings to match demand.

Kate found herself watching the buzz of activity on Main Street; one would stop short of calling it traffic. There were several tree companies and power trucks lumbering past, including McKenna trucks. Her brother and husband pulled up in front of the shop in Shane's pickup truck. Kate figured they were stopping for a quick lunch before heading to the next job.

Donovan Price was the perfect complement to his bride. At six-foot-four, he was powerfully built. His biceps were like tree trunks, and his legs were solid muscle. His dark brown eyes were molten chocolate and permanently crinkled at the corners from spending most days outdoors.

His closely cropped blond hair was bleached white and often covered with a tattered baseball cap. Kate grew weak in the knees every time she saw him. He was the love of her life.

"Hello, love!" Kate leaned in and bussed Don's mouth tenderly. "You're running late today. I thought you might skip lunch since it's getting so late," she teased. "Usually I can set my watch by you."

Shane tweaked her nose. "Sis, we had to fit Mom's house in so we're running a tad behind. So, how about you hand over some of those fresh baked cookies and our lunch and we'll get going. We have trees to cut up, yards to clear. We are busy, hungry men."

Brother and sister enjoyed their playful banter. Losing their dad had created a tightly knit family unit.

At first when Kate asked Don to move with her to Loudon, he had worried about the close proximity of her family. He came from a family of eight who thought every aspect of your personal life was up for discussion or debate. After visiting a few times he discovered the McKennas were respectful of personal space but jumped in when necessary.

Don counted his lucky stars the day he literally bumped into Kate. He had been coming out of an Italian bakery on Fed Hill in Providence. He was more interested in munching on a cannoli than watching where he was going. Kate was strolling down the sidewalk sipping an iced tea, when she was knocked off her feet, drenching her pristine chef coat. Her green eyes shot bolts of lightning at him as he tried, clumsily, to pat her dry. The harder he laughed the madder she got. She stormed off down the street, and he ran after her, pleading for her to stop and begging for her phone number.

Kate shouted back over her shoulder, calling him a jerk before she disappeared into the throng of people on the crowded sidewalk. She didn't want to go out with a clod that couldn't walk down a sidewalk without knocking innocent people over!

Donovan was fascinated by Kate and spent every minute he could spare on Fed Hill, hoping to run into her again. Weeks dragged on when finally on a warm fall day Don found her, sitting on a bench in Fountain Square. Cautiously, he approached, hoping to get her name and number. He had brought a peace offering of iced tea and Italian cookies with the hope he could join her. Don came to a halt in front of her, blocking the sun that was warming her face. Before she had the chance to say anything, he dropped on the bench next to her and apologized profusely for literally running into her the last time they met. She looked at him through squinted eyes, graciously accepted the tea and cookies, and slid over to give him more room on the bench. It was the first time Don believed in love at first sight.

Kate finished packing a hearty lunch and added bottled water from the cooler. "Boys, I packed plenty of water, make sure to drink enough. It's brutally hot today. I know you'll work hard to get the work done, but try to avoid heat exhaustion, please." She lightly kissed her husband, patted her brother's cheek, and shooed them out the door at the end of a snapping towel. "Now I've got work to do so stop hanging around in the air conditioning and get moving." What a pair, she thought, brothers from different mothers, and she was a lucky girl.

Chapter Three

CARI DREADED HEARING THE EXTENT OF THE DAMAGE TO HER HOUSE. She had called the insurance company and a claims adjuster would be out tomorrow. Hopefully it wouldn't take long to get everything finalized.

When she and Ben stumbled on it, the house had been standing vacant for several years and they found it was in sorry shape. The wraparound porch sagged, barely attached to the house. Cari fell in love with the house instantly and told Ben the backyard was perfect for children. Flowers bloomed at the foundation, and a sunroom could replace a poorly built room that jutted off the back. It would be her oasis to read and play piano. It was the kind of house that would be home to their future family. Cari convinced Ben to buy the large rambling Victorian on Maple Street, complete with a weed-filled yard for the budding McKenna family.

The first summer, Cari and Ben planted flowers, shrubs, and trees, and when the weather turned cold, they peeled wallpaper, sanded, and painted woodwork. It took time but eventually her sunroom became a reality. Stepping over the threshold was magical to her. The room was bathed in natural light and she decorated it with floral prints, fairies tucked here and there, overflowing plants, and her piano. When Cari sank into her favorite overstuffed chair, she could let go and relax. It was in that chair she cried a river of tears after Ben died. She didn't know how she would have gotten through the heartbreaking days that followed without her sanctuary.

Cari drove on autopilot, sitting in the car, but lost in the past. She heard a horn toot and noticed Ray had pulled his truck in behind her car. The sound had jarred her back to the present. She had to remind herself that now, her special place was a soggy mess, splinters of wood, and shards of glass. Ray and Shane had done their best to drape the tarp over the hole so the piano was protected but she still had to determine what could be salvaged.

Cari glanced in the rearview mirror, giving a little wave before getting out of the car.

"Hi, Cari. Were you able to get in contact with the insurance agency?"

Ray had driven past the house about an hour before and saw Cari's car parked in the driveway. He figured she was feeling overwhelmed with the idea of facing the cleanup and the rebuilding process. He wanted to wrap his arms around, comfort her, and do his best to reassure her that everything would be fine and the house would be good as new. Instead, he walked to the back of the truck to grab a pad, pencil, and tape measure.

"Come on, let's get started before it's too dark to see what we're talking about. I've been thinking, and I hope you might consider a few changes." Ray wanted his enthusiasm to be contagious.

He saw Cari take a deep breath, and she said, "I have to remind myself that no one got hurt and anything can be fixed. It's just wood and glass."

Ray slowly nodded in agreement. "Okay, see how the tree hit the upper part of the house?" Cari stared at what was left of the house—how could anyone miss the hole? Ray pointed to the roofline and then down to the foundation. "We don't need to worry about the foundation—it's solid. Also, the carrying beam that ties to the main house some-how managed to escape damage. There is no need to be concerned about the main house. We'll need to concentrate on the sunroom, fix the roof and walls, and replace windows. The rain did some damage to the interior so we need to start clearing out what can be saved—furniture, your piano, and anything else—and then we can gut it." Ray glanced at Cari, giving her a minute to absorb the information. "Again, now is the time to make any changes to the space."

"Well, overall it's not as bad as I thought." Cari had been listening closely as Ray gave her the facts.

"We can add more natural light, skylights, larger windows, maybe even a French door that would lead into the flower garden. It would be your space but with a fresh twist. I know you spend a lot of time working in your flowers. It might be nice if you could have easy access to your garden."

"Won't more glass mean my heating bill will sky rocket? We have four months of the year in the deep freeze of New England. I don't want to sit on the sofa in a heavy coat!"

"Of course everything that's installed will have the highest insulation ratings so you don't have to worry. I know the changes might be hard to visualize so I put together a quick sketch of what I think it might look like. It'll give you some idea of the concept." Ray, all business, handed a sketch to Cari.

Cari gasped at the detailed drawings. She was amazed to see Ray's ideas come to life. He had included a fieldstone path that led to the flower garden and wrapped around the sunroom.

"This is incredible, Ray. What else did you do today besides work on this? It's amazing! You created an open floor plan for the room and the garden path is something I've always wanted to do. The French doors open onto the deck. . . ."

She flipped it over and saw that on the drawing of the exterior side Ray had included pots of flowers flowing from the deck, down the stairs, and leading into the gardens. She could picture a couple of lounge chairs on an inviting deck for lazy afternoons.

Ray enjoyed watching her study each page. He knew how much time she spent in the room from all the nights that lights softly glowed from behind curtains. In the summer months, he sat outside in the warm evening air and enjoyed her music. He loved everything she played, mesmerized by soft and sad melodies, rocking country, and, occasionally, a little jazz. Ray wanted to rebuild her oasis and all he needed to get started was for Cari to say yes.

"Well, Cari, to be honest, I had a lot of fun watching my ideas take on a life of their own and designing is my passion. I'm glad you like it," Ray said nonchalantly.

"That's an understatement. I wasn't sure if I'd just fix it, but after seeing your ideas I'm ready to get started."

Ray gathered the stakes he had brought from the truck. "Let's take a walk and stake out the deck so you can see how it would come out toward the flowers. Then you might have some ideas for other things we should add to the project."

Ray saw Cari steal a look at her watch. He didn't want to hold her up. "We should be done in about a half hour and then I'll take off."

"You're not keeping me. I wanted to ask if you'd like to have dinner with me. I have chicken marinating, a tossed salad, and I happen to have some great bread from the shop. We can have a drink and talk about pricing while the chicken grills."

Cari surprised herself; she couldn't believe that she asked Ray to stay for dinner. Except when the kids were around, they had never had dinner before. Now, just because of a couple of pretty drawings, words were popping out of her mouth unchecked. "I'm sure you have other plans so we can talk about estimates later. I appreciate all the work you put into this already."

Amused, Ray let her fumble with her words. Cari was prattling on, her hands going as fast as her pretty mouth. He thought it was cute that she was flustered talking to him, and he enjoyed listening to her. But the bonus, she had asked him to stay for dinner.

"Whoa, Cari, slow down! Let's get some measurements. And dinner sounds great. We can eat and go over figures, too. You should have some idea what it's going to take to fix the house before the insurance guy gets here."

Cari nodded as they walked over to where the tree once stood. "Yes, I have an appointment tomorrow and I'm hoping I can start the cleanup soon. So, what's next?" Cari gave Ray her full attention.

He pointed to a spot next to the house. "Okay, stand here and hold the end of the tape. We'll measure out ten feet, put a stake in the ground, and then do the same ten feet down a ways. Let's see if the deck will be big enough."

Gesturing toward where a double window had been, Ray said, "I think that's the best place for French doors. It already has a header in place. We can build the deck to extend out from both sides of the door. Give some thought as to what would you want to put out here? If you don't think you'll have enough space, now is the time to make it larger. It's easy to move stakes, not so easy to move concrete pillars."

Cari helped hammer stakes into the ground, and the outline took shape. She could visualize how it would look. Ray had captured the essence of her home, infusing it with new energy.

"I'm sold on the idea but one thing is bothering me." Cari glanced at the future deck outline.

"I overlooked something?" Ray shook his head. Typically, his drawings were right on target.

"I think if I'm going to have lounge chairs, potted flowers and plants, the deck is going to need to be wider and a little deeper. Also, I might want to add a small table and chairs for dining al fresco. So," Cari turned to smile up at him, "can we make it bigger?"

He grinned at her. "Sure, let's move the stakes to where you think it makes sense and then take final measurements."

Ray spent years thinking she needed a deck surrounded by flowers. It was the perfect complement to the house. He could never tell her these ideas had been running around in his head for years.

"Well," she teased, "I guess if you've been looking at

someone's backyard for over twenty years the ideas might have been gelling for a while." She gave his shirt a playful tug. "The grill is calling, let's go and have some dinner. I don't know about you but I'm starving."

Ray was stunned she seemed to have read his mind. He trailed after Cari, admiring the backside of her form-fitting jeans.

Ray leaned over the chopping block in her kitchen, watching her efficiently chop vegetables for salad. "What can I do to help?"

"I've got this covered. Maybe you can set the table? The plates are in the cupboard to the right of the sink. Silverware is in the top drawer and glasses are in the cupboard to the left."

Ray did as requested and set the small table by the large window overlooking the backyard. He said, "I didn't realize you had such a large vegetable garden. Where do you find the time to run the shop, keep the yard looking well manicured, and flower gardens popping up everywhere?"

"It's something I love to do and there's nothing better in the winter than pulling pickles off the shelf that you put up or making spaghetti sauce from tomatoes grown in the summer. It's the fresh taste of summer all year long." She grinned.

Ray said, "You know I don't know if I have ever had sauce from homegrown tomatoes. My ex-wife served pre-packed, processed everything, or take out."

"Well, sometime this winter I'll make a batch and invite you over, you'll never want to eat sauce from a jar again," Cari said as she flashed him a knowing smile.

Chapter Four

THE INSURANCE ADJUSTER HAD LEFT, and Cari came to a decision on the drive to the shop. It didn't matter what the insurance company would pay, she was going with Ray's plan for the sunroom. Fortunately, Ben had provided for her and the kids, and the shop did a steady business. Cari wasn't rich but she had always lived on a budget and had more than enough tucked away to do whatever she wanted.

It felt odd walking into the shop midmorning. It was the first lull of the day when a few young mothers enjoyed quiet time while their little ones were in nursery school at a nearby church. Cari gave them a jaunty wave and stepped behind the counter. As usual, she tied her apron on, pulled her hair off her face, and went looking for Kate.

"Kate, I'm back! It didn't take as long as I thought," she called out.

"Hey, Mom!" Kate was carrying a bowl of sliced apples over to the center workstation. "You're all set with the insurance company?"

Cari reached over to steal an apple slice. "Yes."

"Did Ray stop over last night?"

Kate couldn't help but notice her mom's smile was enhanced by a touch of lip color in addition to her usual makeup.

"Ray came over after work and showed me his drawings. They're wonderful! I had no idea he could draw like that. I was amazed at the level of detail he put into them. He suggested adding French doors, a deck, and opening up the interior with larger windows." Her words tumbled out in a rush of excitement. "And over dinner we talked about a few more details."

"The two of you had dinner together?" Kate struggled to keep a straight face. She would have to do some verbal tap dancing to find out if anything else happened.

"After we talked about material costs, he casually mentioned he had talked to Shane, Don, and Jake. They're going to work with him to keep labor costs down. I told him I couldn't accept their generous offer and that unless I paid the standard hourly rate I would have to find another builder."

Kate couldn't keep quiet. "Mom, I don't think Ray meant anything by asking the guys to help. You know that Shane and Don will be swinging a hammer whether Ray asked them or not. Jake has been an honoree member of our family forever. Shane and Jake were inseparable as kids. With that long history, I'm sure he wants to help. Some of these changes you want might be expensive, and I happen to think it was very sweet of him. "

Cari stewed for a few minutes. "Well, you could be right. Ray thought he was being funny when he told me it was going to cost me more in food, drinks, and snacks than labor because the boys can eat more than their weight so he'd be getting a better deal."

Kate finished slicing the apples, tossed them with sugar and cinnamon, and spooned them into the waiting tart crust. She focused on the tart in an attempt to cover her laughter. Did her mother forget that when a guy likes a girl he tries to impress her? How could Kate open her mom's eyes to see what was going on right in front of her?

"Sounds like things are moving right along. Any idea when you can start the cleanup?"

"If I had my way we'd get started today. Can you check with Don, and I'll talk to Shane? Let's see if we can get arrange something on Saturday. The adjuster took lots of pictures. I'll call tomorrow and ask if we can get started. Maybe we should turn it into a party. I'll call Ray, hopefully Jake and Sara can come, too."

Cari mumbled under her breath, "I'm going to start time sheets to make sure everyone gets paid for the time they put in."

Kate didn't hear her mother talking to herself but piped up, "That sounds like a great idea. We'll make some of the food tomorrow. You can count on us, and I can call Ellie."

"I'll say something to her when she gets home tonight, or maybe leave her a note. Heaven knows she's on her own schedule. I never know if she's coming or going."

Kate couldn't wait to observe her mom and Ray together. Something was definitely in the air.

Shane and Don came strolling in when the shop was bustling. Cari was waiting on someone so they wandered into the kitchen in search of Kate.

"Hey, sis, what's cooking?" He reached underneath her arm and grabbed a piece of freshly sliced cheese.

Kate slapped his hand. "Don't reach under the slicer. Do you want to lose a hand? Bloody cheese isn't good for business."

Kate turned her face up to her husband, waiting for a kiss. "Hi, sweetheart. Did you have anything you wanted to do on Saturday?"

Don shook his head. "Nope. Did you want to do something?"

"Mom wants to clean up the tree damage on Saturday, and Ray's going to start construction as soon as the insurance people give the go ahead. Oh, I hear Ray talked to you about helping out with the construction?"

Contentedly munching on sliced cheese and turkey, Shane shrugged his shoulders. "Yeah, he said something the other night that he'd be happy for help and if we all pitch in he thinks it will be done before the snow flies. We've got some room in our schedule in the next few weeks so I told him it wasn't a problem. I talked to Jake and he's in, too. So we're cool."

"Mom does a lot for us so we can give up some weekends too if necessary," Don added.

Nodding in agreement, Kate said, "I can help, too. I've gotten pretty good with a hammer now that we've finished our house. But, Shane, don't you think it's a little odd that Ray doesn't want to get paid? That's going to be a lot of hours. I mean, we're family but what about Jake and Ray?"

"Kate, it's no big deal. We live in a small town and you know everyone helps each other when they can. Besides, Mom and Ray have been friends for a long time. Relax, sis, it's all good."

Exasperated, Kate thought Shane couldn't see what was going on right under his nose.

"Kate, we gotta get going, would you throw some sandwiches together for your hubby and favorite brother?" Shane was anxious to get back to the job they were working on. "I left Tom Hamlin in charge, and I'm sure he thinks we've gotten lost. Actually, can you throw in extra? I don't want to listen to him grumble that he's dying of starvation. The next time he'll want to do the lunch run." Shane gave his sister's cheek a pinch.

"Okay, you win. Will two sandwiches be enough for each of you?" Shane grabbed the bag as soon as Kate slid in the sandwiches.

Don pulled his wife into his arms and gave her a lingering kiss before following Shane. "See you tonight, love," he called.

"Water! You never drink enough," she reminded them.

"You're the best. Talk to you later." Shane slipped past his mom, grabbed a few cookies, gave her a glancing peck, and was gone.

"Kate, did you did ask the boys about Saturday?"

"We'll all be there. I haven't called Ellie. She'll be out of class shortly and I'll ask if she can swing by tomorrow and help get some food ready." Kate wiped down the counter and pondered the next item on her agenda: her mother's love life.

For the remainder of the day, Kate was quiet but Cari didn't notice. Cari welcomed each customer with a warm smile and served cold drinks and sweet treats. Most were regulars and a few stopped to socialize. Some folks lived alone and this might be the only human contact they had for the day. Cari was pleased What's Perkin' was a local hangout and everyone was welcome to come and linger.

As the afternoon sun shone in the windows, Cari flipped the closed sign on the door and pulled up a stool to sit down and have a bite to eat. "Katelyn, are you feeling okay? You've been quiet all afternoon. Is there something you want talk about?"

Kate came in from the kitchen and looked directly at Cari. "Have you ever considered dating? Getting out in the world to see if you can find someone and maybe fall in love?"

Cari was stunned. It was a good thing she was sitting down otherwise she would have fallen over. Cari studied her daughter, wondering where this was coming from.

Did the kids think she was unfulfilled or unhappy? She missed Ben but she didn't feel lonely, well, at least not often. Cari felt he was still with her and they communicated.

The silence was deafening. Kate thought she might have overstepped her boundaries.

"Kate, do you think I'm unhappy?" Cari spoke softly. "I love my life. I have my home and gardens. I have a good business that keeps me busy, and I get to spend time with you, Ellie, and Shane. I have amazing friends. I do charity work that makes me happy—Kate, I am truly blessed. I don't think I could ask for anything more than what I have."

"I know that you are busy, but Dad has been gone a long time, Mom. I think he would want for you to have someone special. He would understand," she said quietly.

Kate chose her next words very carefully, unsure if her mom was ready for his brilliant idea. "Do you think there might be a reason why the tree fell on the house? Wasn't it one that Daddy planted? Maybe it's him trying to push you to make some changes. Deep down I know Dad wouldn't want you to be eating dinner alone almost every night.

We've grown up and are starting our lives, just like you both dreamed we would. But it's time you had someone to share your life with."

Cari heard what Kate was saying but was surprised the kids wanted her to have a man.

"Honey, I know he's gone. I was lucky to have him in my life, and he gave me three wonderful children. I can't imagine anyone filling his shoes."

"I don't think you should try to fill his shoes, but what about a different set of shoes? Would you like to have someone as part of your life, where you can do things as part of a couple? Go away for a romantic weekend or go on a picnic to the lake, a bicycle built for two." Kate paused to let that sink in.

"I didn't know you kids felt like this." Cari shifted uncomfortably on the stool. "Just when I think I read you like an open book I still find a surprise tucked inside."

Cari slipped off the stool and squeezed her daughter tight. "Even if I wanted to date, how do I go about meeting someone? It's not like I'm a college girl with guys everywhere and roller rinks are out of business. So, how does a woman my age date?"

"Have you ever thought of Internet dating?" Kate said cautiously, hoping her mom would consider it. "It's like shopping for a guy but online."

"What, you want me to look for a date on the Internet?" Cari didn't know whether to laugh or tell Kate to forget about the whole idea.

Partially amused, she said, "I guess you can find just about anything on the Internet these days. Kate, I promise to give it some thought, fair enough?"

Kate turned away from her mom, pretending she needed to tidy something in the display case. She wanted to dance a jig but instead she said, "Ellie and I can help you set up your online profile and get a couple of good pictures to add, when you're ready."

"Kate, stop pushing. I said I'd think about it. In the meantime let's get back to something productive, like what are we going to serve Saturday?" Skillfully, Cari moved the conversation back to safe ground.

Kate thought the dating conversation went better than expected. Maybe there was hope yet, and after a couple of bad dates, Cari would open her eyes and see who was in her own backyard.

Cari pulled over the legal pad to jot down the shopping list for Saturday. However, she was distracted by the idea of Internet dating. Her last first date had been more than twenty-eight years ago. How does a person go about choosing an Internet dating site? It's enough to boggle her mind. She was definitely out of her comfort zone. Shopping for clothes was one thing, but a man? Bizarre!

"Don't forget to buy plenty to drinks, including beer, Mom. Let's make this a party instead of just work." Kate stole the pen out of her mom's hand and in bold letters wrote BEER!

"Hello?" Cari's youngest daughter called out as the door banged shut, making her usual grand entrance.

Over the years, Cari had said she should have named her Grace instead of Eleanor. She was always knocking things over, tripping over her feet, and spilling whatever she ate or drank. It was beyond Cari to understand how someone who was just barely five feet tall could always make an entrance like a force of nature.

"Hey, baby girl." Cari hugged her little pixie. "What brings you by today? Were your ears ringing because we were just talking about you?"

Ellie's sapphire blue eyes sparkled like jewels. "You were? I hope you were only saying good things. Like I am the most amazing, smart, and talented daughter you have," she teased. "Oh, Kate, I'm so sorry I didn't see you standing there."

"Hey, squirt. You saw me, you're just being a brat like usual." Kate tugged Ellie's sleek, short blond hair.

The girls were a sharp contrast to each other, dark to fair, and tall to short. However, both could turn heads. Their features had strong similarities, leaving no doubt they were sisters.

"Ouch, that hurts! Mom, will you tell Katie to stop messing up my hair!"

Cari loved watching the girls go through the same routine for years. By the time Ellie was walking, Kate had grown into her long legs. Ellie had to work hard to keep up with her and Shane. It was Ellie who was born at a dead run.

"Oh girls, are you going to do this till you're old and gray?" Amused, Cari pulled both their hair.

Kate and Ellie answered in unison with big silly grins, "Yup, old but never gray!"

Ellie swiped the half of a sandwich that was sitting on the plate. She pulled up a stool to sit with her mother and sister.

"So, what were you talking about before I showed up?" Ellie asked between bites.

"I hope you don't have plans for Saturday. We've asked a bunch of people to come over and help clean up the debris left by the tree falling on the house. Ray worked up a new design, which Mom loves, so he and the boys are going to get started on the construction. So, of course we should turn it into a party."

"Yeah, I'll see who I can round up. Just make sure you have enough food and drink, the guys can really eat. What time are we getting started?" Ellie pulled out her phone and started texting people. She paused midtext, waiting for an answer.

"Let's say nine." Cari added a few more things to her list. "I'll put out some muffins and such to start with."

"Done." Ellie slid her phone into her pocket and polished off the sandwich. "So, what else is going on?" Ellie looked from Kate to Cari.

"Mom is thinking about setting up an online profile for

Internet dating. She might put a toe in and test the waters," Kate announced.

Ellie wasn't totally surprised by the news, it's what she and Kate had talked about for a long time. "That's awesome, Mom! My friend Krissy, her mom is dating online. I can find out which one she's using and you can check it out. Don't forget you'll need pictures, too."

Cari got the feeling she had been set up. It sounded like the girls had talked about Internet dating between themselves prior to this conversation. She had to wonder who else the girls had been talking to. Most likely Grace was in on this, too. Oh well, she thought, what did she have to lose? It might even turn out to be fun.

Chapter Five

CARI SAT AT THE KITCHEN TABLE STARING AT THE SCREEN ON HER LAPTOP. How does a person go about choosing a dating site? she muttered to herself. To her surprise, a quick search turned up more websites than she would have guessed. Depending upon what she was looking for, all types were listed for her perusal. She had seen ads for Matchmaker, Single and 30+, and Are You the One? Cari logged onto a site and read the testimonials from people who had found their soul mates. It's like window-shopping, but instead of shoes, it's men, she thought.

Resting her chin on her hand, she stared at the screen. "Hmmm, how do I choose one? If I'm going to humiliate myself, maybe signing up for a couple will increase my odds." Cari looked across the table to the empty chair.

"Ben, I wish you were here so I could ask your opinion."

Sometimes the void she felt was like a wool blanket in summer, wrapped so tight she couldn't breathe.

"Cari, I'm always with you." Cari glanced up from the keyboard to see Ben smiling at her from the once-vacant chair.

"I guess when I need you the most, you come." Sadly, Cari knew that his visit, like all of them, wouldn't be long enough.

"Ben, am I doing the right thing? When I think about dating I feel like I'm betraying you."

"Cari, our love didn't die, I did. It's time for you to move on and shake things up around here. When I pop in I don't see that you're moving forward, not really, and it's time, my darling. In your heart, you know it's time to create a place in your life for someone special. I don't want you to be alone. For the past fifteen years, you've done a great job being both mother and father to our kids, but now it's time for you. It's not like you're pushing up daisies, too."

Tears streamed down her cheeks. She knew he was right, but she didn't want to let go. "It's hard for me to accept that I have to live my life without you. We were supposed to grow old together."

"It's time for you to find someone who is able to grow old with you and not be a dream of what should have been."

Cari bent her head down to wipe the tears away. When she looked up, Ben's chair was empty. It had been a long time since he had come to talk with her even though she talked to him daily. Somewhere in her heart she knew why the tree fell, but did Ben have to destroy her favorite part of the house to prove a point?

"Okay, Ben, I got the message. Time for me to move on. But I will always love you."

Softly, like hummingbird wings, she heard "And I you." And then, silence.

Cari got up and poured herself a glass of chilled white wine. She sat down and faced her computer, fingers poised on the keys. Taking a deep breath, she dove into creating a dating profile.

Laughing out loud, she finished her vital statistics. She had to select the basic criteria for what she was looking for in a man. Age . . . five years older and five years younger. That sounded reasonable. Then, how far did she want to travel for a date? Okay, thirty-mile radius. And she'd need to see their pictures. Camera shy, no need to contact this girl!

She hit the enter button and found there were 127 men that fit her "must haves." Well, where were they all hiding? Cari didn't think there were 127 decent men in the northeast.

Holding her hand above the button to submit her personal profile, she took a deep breath and . . . click. She paused for a few minutes wondering what she had just done.

Was this how single people really met? Her e-mail dinged, announcing new mail had arrived. Curious she checked. It was from the Single website. Wow, she thought, that was fast. Clicking the link, she saw there was a message from Ray. She opened up the e-mail and laughed as she read,

Welcome to dating the 21st-century style.

She sent a quick response of thanks and signed off. She never would have guessed that he would have trouble meeting women. He was gorgeous and possibly the nicest man she knew. Her grandmother had always said there was a pot for every lid and maybe the Internet was the best place to shop for one. Smiling, Cari shut down and headed to bed. The next two days were going to be very busy. A good night's sleep was in order.

Saturday dawned sunny and hot. Cari pulled on jeans, work boots, and a short-sleeved tee and pulled her ponytail through the back of her purple cap. She stepped out into the bright sun, ready to set out tables and coolers. The girls baked a variety of cookies and muffins along with a fruit tray for breakfast. No one would go hungry, she thought. Later they'd grill burgers, hot dogs, chicken wings, and various other picnic foods. Satisfied, she was anxious to get started with the heavy work.

Shane had arranged for a construction dumpster to be delivered for the debris and he promised to bring rakes, shovels, and wheelbarrows, too.

Before long, she heard trucks rumbling in the driveway and the buzz of chatter. She walked around to greet her family and was amazed to see the driveway overflowing with people, including the guys who worked for Shane.

Shane walked over and slung his arm around Cari's shoulder. "Mom, we thought if we got a bunch of people to help out today we could get done quicker and then just hang around, eat, and relax. I didn't think you'd mind." Turning to the group, he yelled, "Hey, can ya'll grab the tools off the back of my truck? And there are a bunch of wheelbarrows on the trailer."

Cari stood rooted to the spot, watching as tools were unloaded and everyone moved towards the backyard. "I hope we have enough food. . . ." Cari muttered.

"Ray said he would be here in a little bit. He had a quick stop to make," Shane called back over his shoulder.

"Before you get started, grab a muffin and something to drink," Cari called out to the people swarming around the yard.

The guys obliged as they walked by the table and grabbed muffins, munching as they walked toward the house. Cari was pulling on her work gloves when she caught sight of Ray walking around the garage pushing a wheelbarrow that carried some sort of tree. Curious, Cari headed in his direction.

"Hi, Cari!" Ray grinned. "I thought since you lost a tree in the storm maybe you'd want to replace it. It's a pink flowering dwarf crab apple. I noticed you have a white one in the front yard and you planted flowers at the base so I thought you might like one in the back, too. If you'd like we can plant some bulbs this fall, and you can have color early in the spring and then add annuals for the summer."

Cari was touched by the gesture. "Ray, I appreciate your thoughtfulness but you didn't need to buy me a tree. I'm sure it was expensive, you'll have to let me pay for it."

Ray was irritated and mildly amused at the same time. "Cari, I didn't buy it so you could reimburse me. I bought it because I thought you'd like it. You cooked a fantastic dinner the other night, and you have to admit the week wasn't exactly the best with the tree falling. Can you just say 'thank you' and we can get to work?"

Cari hadn't meant to offend him. She wasn't used to receiving gifts and wasn't sure how to react. "I'm sorry, Ray. I'm not sure what I was thinking. Thank you, I didn't mean to sound ungrateful. This variety is one of my favorites, and now I have one in front and in back."

Ray smiled at Cari still holding the wheelbarrow handles. "Where should I put this so it doesn't get in the way?"

Cari pointed to the side door. "It should be safe over there." Ray hauled the tree out of the wheelbarrow and plopped it down. For the first time, he noticed the table full of food.

"Did you make coffee, too?" His blue eyes twinkled.

"Of course," Laughing, she crossed to the pot, pumped a cup of steaming coffee, and handed it to him. "Cream and sugar are right there. Help yourself."

Cari went to join the group working, and Ray chomped on a muffin while enjoying the view as she walked away, ponytail bouncing slightly. Cari's jeans hugged her curves but she didn't have that poured into them look. Smiling to himself, he said, "It's going to be an interesting day."

Everyone worked quickly to move the small debris and any furniture that could be salvaged. Broken windows and sharp objects were raked into flat shovels and relocated into the dumpster. As the morning evaporated, the temperature rose and the room became a shell of wooden beams.

Ray and Jake looked up as they finished hauling the last chunk of tree out of the middle of the room.

"Hey, Cari. We're starting to fade away. Any chance for a snack?"

"Lunch is coming up in about a half hour?" she replied.

Despite dripping with sweat, smudges of dirt on his face, and his T-shirt plastered to his chest, Ray's usual smile lit up his face. "Great!"

Jake's wife Sara came up to her. "Cari, what can I do to help?"

"Do you want to pull the platters out of the refrigerator? Also, I have salads, a tray of burger fixings, and whatever else you think should come out. I'm going to light the grill and start cooking wings, they're in the cooler with the burgers and hot dogs."

Cari looked up to see if Kate and Ellie could assist with grill duty. Kate was wandering in the direction of the grill but Ellie was busy chatting up Dave, one of the guys from her college. Cari felt sorry for him. Ellie didn't know how to control her flirtatious nature. Cari had doubts this would develop into anything more than friendship either. Ellie wasn't interested in a steady guy. She dated occasionally, but she said she'd know when the right one came along. Until then, she had plenty of friends.

Kate grilled, stacking burgers, chicken, and dogs on platters. The tables were full with every kind of food imaginable. If anyone left hungry it was his or her own fault. While Kate encouraged everyone to eat, she watched Cari slip away for a quiet moment.

Ray kept an eye on Cari from behind dark glasses. He hoped the new space would give her the peace and security she craved. He knew Cari well enough to understand she needed to get comfortable with the idea of change. He longed to walk up behind her and take her in his arms. He wondered if there would ever come a day when he'd be able to hold her, run his hands through the thick dark waves of her hair and down her back. The desire to be near her was so strong he couldn't stop himself. He crossed the lawn in a few long strides and silently walked up behind her.

Cari felt Ray standing behind her but she didn't want him to see the tears threatening to spill from her eyes. He might mistake them for sadness, when the opposite was true. Looking at the empty space, for the first time she felt excited about the change that had already taken place. When it was done, her family would fill the room with new memories. Before she turned to face him, she discreetly rubbed the back of her hand across her eyes. She hoped Ray missed the subtle gesture.

Ray reached out and touched her arm. "Cari, why are you sad? What can I do to help?"

"Ray, your drawings, my house, it's going to be amazing." Cari turned to him, her eyes shining. She threw her arms around him and gave him a bear hug. "Thank you for everything. I know there is a lot of work to do but I can see what you see."

Taken aback, Ray squeezed her tight and then stepped back.

"Cari, it's what I do: create something from a dream or idea. It's like going into the woods after a fire and new shoots are pushing up from the charred remains, reaching toward the sky with new possibilities. This project is important to me, too. I want to be able to look out my kitchen window and know that you're happy in your home. Everyone needs to have a place where they can retreat from the world."

Cari's smile warmed his heart. "Ray, I don't know how you did it, but you managed to take the ideas right out of my head and put them on paper even before I knew what I wanted. You are bringing my dream to reality. I will never be able to tell you how much this means to me."

Cari reached out and hugged him again. The scent of her shampoo teased his nose. She stepped back and squeezed his hand. "Let's get something to eat before it's all gone."

After all these years, two hugs and a squeeze of the hand and he was a goner. He knew, without a doubt, what he wanted was to spend the rest of his life with Cari in his arms and by his side.

Cari was a half second behind him. A mental picture flashed in her head: walking hand in hand with Ray down a tree-lined dirt road. She shook her head from side to side in an attempt to clear her head, thinking, he's a good friend. You start Internet dating and all of a sudden, you start daydreaming about him. What's next, night dreams, too? She laughed out loud and fell in step beside him not giving the idea a second thought.

Kate and Ellie had witnessed the exchange between their mom and Ray. "Did you see what I saw?" Ellie asked grinning.

"Where have you been, Pixie? Why do you think I want Mom to start Internet dating?"

Exasperated, Ellie looked at Kate. "If you want her to date Ray then why are you encouraging her to sign up for Internet dating? That's about the dumbest thing you've said in a long time!"

"Ellie, Ray has been a family friend for years. Mom has never noticed he's a hottie and living right next door. All she sees is her friend and loyal customer. She needs to wake up and see that he gets this look on his face every time they're together, like she hung the moon or something. I've been watching whatever this is simmer since I got back, and I think it's been going on a lot longer than any of us would guess."

"Really, you think Ray has a thing for Mom?" Ellie was dumbfounded. "So, if you think Ray has a thing for Mom, and Mom has a thing for Ray, then why Internet dating? I'm confused."

Confidently, Kate announced, "You're missing the obvious. If Mom sees the kind of guys that troll dating sites and goes on a few bad dates, I know she'll open her eyes and see what is standing right in front of her at seven sharp every morning."

"Oh, I get it. Reverse psychology or something, right? How did you come up with it?" Ellie nodded, grinning. "Great idea, sis."

Finally, Kate thought, the light bulb went off above her sister's head. "You need to come down to the shop some morning and watch these two. She lights up when he walks in and doesn't even realize it. You know that saying 'sometimes you can't see the forest for the trees'? Well, Mom can't see the best tree is right in her backyard."

"Do you think she's ready, Katie? Dad's been gone a long time, but their relationship has been everything to her, maybe she thinks you only deserve to get that once in a lifetime."

Kate brushed a lock of hair off her sister's forehead and placed a hand softly on her cheek.

Kate paused. "Ellie, I think when you experience a connection that profound, you're able to recognize it again.

Deep and steadfast love is extremely rare, and it's like nothing else on earth. I think Mom will find it again, and she'll recognize and appreciate it when she does." In one fluid motion, Kate hugged Ellie with one arm and tugged her hair. "And someday, Pixie, you'll find it, too.

Let's get things finished up. Tomorrow, we can concentrate on nudging Mom into Ray's arms."

Chapter Six

STANDING AT THE COUNTER WITH HER LAPTOP OPEN, Cari was reading her e-mail. She was curious to see if she had any matches and surprised to discover seventeen unread messages. Potential dates? she wondered. Cari imagined what was beyond the first click. The shop was quiet and curiosity got the best of her, so she opened the first link and chuckled.

"Mom," Kate shouted from the back, "what are you laughing at?"

"Nothing I'm just doing a little shopping and saw something funny."

Cari wasn't sure if she wanted to share that she had a bunch of hits on her profile.

Kate came out of the back, wiping her hands on the towel. "Let me see what's so funny. Push over." Kate hip bumped her mom to one side. Peering at the screen, Kate could see her mother had a bunch of new e-mails.

Peering over Cari's shoulder, Kate exclaimed, "The dating site?"

"Yes. Can you believe that many people read my profile?" Cari said.

This was a double-edged sword as far as Kate was concerned. She was glad her mom had a great response, but she hoped they were all duds. The real gem had already been at the shop a couple of hours earlier.

"We should check a couple of these out." Kate grabbed two mugs of coffee, splashed in some cream, and walked over to a table that faced the front window. Kate wanted to keep an eye on the sidewalk. They didn't need customers walking in and overhearing the conversation. It was a small town, and no one needed to know what they were looking at on the computer.

Scrolling through the e-mails, Cari had a running commentary. "I don't think so." Click. "Nope," she said as she hit the Delete button.

"Whoa, hold on, Mom. At least one of these has to be of some interest." Kate pulled the laptop from her mom.

Kate scrolled back to the top. "Okay, I guess someone didn't realize you stated you were interested in men—delete. Some guys must e-mail every new profile. You have nothing in common with most of these."

Cari pointed at the screen. "What about that one? Open it up again, and let's take a look. He posted pictures. If they can't post a relatively recent picture, I'm not going to waste my time."

Kate read the only e-mail that had a remote possibility of potential.

"Okay, so his name's Al, and he's about five years older than you. He's retired from the Marines, no kids, no pets, he likes to garden and ride motorcycles. This picture is kind of far away so you can't really tell what his face looks like, but you can see that he seems to be in decent shape. If that's his bike, it's a nice Harley."

Kate turned the computer so Cari could get a better view. "What do you think?"

Cari thought the guy didn't spark a lot of interest for her. But what did she expect from a brief online profile? "Not bad, let's send him a poke and see if he will e-mail me. I'm not giving out my phone number to anyone until I'm comfortable." She may not have dated in forever but she did know how to play it cool. She'd been watching her girls for a long time.

"What do you want to choose for the poke: 'Hey, nice picture', 'Howdy', 'What's going on?' or a simple smiley face?"

Cari didn't have to think about it. "Just send the smiley face—friendly but nothing over the top."

Cari was curious about Ray's profile.

"You know, Ray has a profile. He pinged me the night I joined, welcoming me to the dating pool. Do you think we should check it out?"

"Well, of course," Kate agreed.

Kate thought this was an interesting turn of events. What was Ray doing on a dating site when a blind person could see he had a thing for her mom? Well, she couldn't blame him. How would he know if he had a shot at being more than friends with Cari after all these years?

A few clicks later, Kate found his profile. "Mom, take a look at this picture, it's incredible." Kate watched her mother slowly read his profile and study the pictures he had posted.

Cari sat mesmerized. His eyes were crystal blue and the contrast of his dark hair was jaw-dropping. Did he really look this handsome? She'd have to pay closer attention. She slowly scrolled through the other photos—Ray with Gifford, and his flower gardens.

Kate continued to observe her mom as she studied Ray's profile. Cari's eyebrows arched with surprise. She smiled as she read his interests, and her eyes kept sliding back his profile picture.

"Kate, it says here that he loves to cook. If that's true, I wonder why he stops in here every day for breakfast and lunch. Well, maybe he thinks frozen pizza is cooking."

Hmm, Kate thought. Cari was glued to the screen, oblivious of everything around her.

"Mom, you might want to cut him some slack, he could be a great cook."

With flushed cheeks Cari glanced at her daughter. With a quick jab on the Escape button, she closed the cover and slid it into her shoulder bag.

"We should get ready for the lunch crowd," she announced. When she had a quiet moment from her nosy but lovable daughter she would have another look at Mr. Ray Davis.

Kate and Cari got back to work and wrapped up a busy day, which led into a busy week. Online dating took a backseat to the demolition of the sunroom.

A few weeks later, Cari was watching the framing process as the room slowly took shape. She wanted Ray to incorporate operable skylights, which hadn't been part of the original design. It had taken more than a month to get the insurance paperwork resolved and another week before they finally got started with construction. Over the last month, Shane ground up the pine's stump and Cari planted the new tree on the edge of the garden where she could see it from the house, where it would complement the riot of color that burst forth each summer. Ray had stopped over a few times to ask questions about the deck and had the wood delivered. He wanted everything ready for when they could start work.

One afternoon Ray strolled into the shop looking for Cari. The shop was empty except for Kate, who was in the middle of baking something that made his mouth water.

"Hello there," Kate smiled warmly. "I haven't seen much of you since we did the demolition."

Returning the smile he said, "You're hard at work when I stop by in the mornings." Ray thought, if he had a daughter, she would be like Kate—friendly, sweet, and warm. "Is your mom around? We've started some interior work and I wanted to show her what we've started. If she wants to make any changes, we should make them now. Changes are costly if we have to go back and rip something out later."

"Sorry, Ray, she went to the bank and then was calling it a day. She's been tired lately. I think the stress is getting to her. I have to admit, I'm glad she took the afternoon off. I'm hoping she'll relax for a while."

Disappointment flashed over Ray's face.

"But," Kate said hastily, "I'm sure she'll be home soon, why don't you stop over?" Kate was dying to tell him to high tail it to the house. An innocent suggestion was okay, she thought.

"Well, if you don't think she'd mind. I'll head over there and, if she's not already there, I'll wait." Ray made a beeline for the door.

Ray slid his sunglasses on and walked into the glare of the sun. He changed direction and made a detour to Hops n' Grapes at the other end of Main Street. He'd pick up a bottle of chilled white wine and a six-pack. Maybe he could convince Cari to have dinner with him. Whistling tunelessly, he headed home.

Cari stopped at the bank and then stopped at Blake's Farmers Market for salad fixings, fresh fish, and dessert. She thought if Ray were around that maybe he'd like to have dinner with her. They could talk about the house and she could pick his brain about Internet dating. She hadn't been overly thrilled with the men who had e-mailed her. Some had been downright rude.

Cari pulled into her driveway. She caught sight of Ray going into his shop. Hurriedly, she put the groceries away and wandered over to see what he was up to.

Running a hand over her hair, she crossed the lawn and she couldn't help but notice the sunroom was taking shape. It looked like it should be weather-tight soon. Fall in New England was a little dicey. There were two possibilities, Indian summer or rain. In her opinion, the sooner it was closed in, the better. She hoped it would be finished before the holidays. With a bounce in her step, she pushed open the door, knocking as she went.

"Hello?"

The smell of freshly cut wood, paint, and stain hung heavy in the air with the underlying scent of a wood fire. Glancing around, she could see door-less cabinets standing to one side and what she assumed were upper cabinets in various stages of completion. The shop was spotless; the floor swept clean and tools were stored but within easy access. Cari had never ventured into Ray's domain and she was intrigued to see the tools and machinery. She had no idea what any of them were used for, but, always curious, she would ask Ray about them all.

"Hello, Cari. This is a surprise." Cari turned to see Ray holding a small piece of wood in his hands. "Did you see the progress at your place?"

"Hi yourself. I did and everything is looking good, well, at least to my untrained eye," she teased. "I don't know how you manage to get everything done at my place when you're building cabinets. It makes me wish I needed some, they're wonderful!"

"Cari, stop, you'll embarrass me. Anyone can build something if they really want to. It takes patience and time but it's pretty easy."

"I don't agree. You have talent, Ray. Is it okay if I look around your shop? I've never seen most of these tools. Do you really use all of them?" Cari looked at one machine, puzzled. "This looks like a huge pasta maker.

Ray let loose a deep belly laugh. "No one has ever said that before. It's called a planer. Rough planks of wood are fed through the rollers and that makes them thinner and creates a smooth finish. Sometimes, if I'm lucky, I can get my hands on old barn boards. I like building furniture out of something that is that old, so this machine comes in handy. Back in the day they had to plane the boards by hand but it's not something I'd want to do."

"Fascinating. How did you learn to use these tools?"

"My dad was a carpenter. When I was a kid I tagged along, and he was a good teacher. I never wanted to do anything else. I would like to build furniture full time but there isn't as much demand as there is for general contractors, so I do custom furniture and cabinetry, incorporating them into projects." He was pleased Cari was interested in his work. "Would you like to try and build something, a bird feeder or something small?"

The words popped out of Ray's mouth. Wishing he could take them back, he stuttered, "That was a stupid idea, never mind." He thought, she wasn't the kind of girl to hang out in a dusty, smelly shop.

"I would love to," she gushed. "What could I build—a cabinet, table, or a bookcase?" Her eyes shined and enthusiasm bubbled over as she continued. "I've never built anything in my life!"

"Hold on a minute. Let's start with something easy, maybe a small knick-knack shelf. Some straight lines are best to start with, and I could help you use a small scroll saw to cut decorative brackets. You can fasten it together and paint or stain it."

Impulsively, Cari threw her arms around Ray, squeezing him tight. "What do we need and when can we start?"

Amused, he said, "You need to think about size, what kind of wood, and if you'll wood stain or paint. These are all important details to make before we go to the lumberyard. I'll need to check on your door and windows next week, do you want to tag along?"

It took Cari a half second to decide, "Count me in. Midweek is best and if you give me twenty-four hours' warning I'll make sure Kate can cover the shop."

"Okay then, it's a . . ." Ray had almost said "date." But he didn't want Cari to get the wrong idea, and he didn't want to make her uncomfortable thinking he had somehow coerced her into a date.

Oblivious that Ray didn't finish his sentence she said, "Sure, you let me know and I'll be ready." For a brief moment Cari felt odd, planning to do something with Ray. It wasn't a date or anything, she reassured herself.

"Well, I'm sure you're wondering why I came busting in today? I wanted to ask if you'd like to have dinner with me. I thought you could bring me up-to-date regarding the sunroom. Also, to be honest, I'd like to pick your brain about this Internet dating thing. I'm a little embarrassed to be asking for dating tips; however, you're the only person I know who's had experience with it. That is, if I'm not getting too personal."

Caught off guard he hesitated for a nanosecond. "That sounds good, and I'm happy to give you some tips for dating in the twenty-first century."

Ray couldn't believe she was asking him for advice. Honestly, he didn't want to give her tips so she could have a better chance of meeting someone. But that would be purely selfish of him. They weren't dating, they were friends. She should go out and have some fun.

Glancing at her watch, Cari said, "Come over in about forty-five minutes. That will give me time to put the salad together and heat the grill. I picked up some salmon."

"Perfect. I'll bring the drinks and some cheese and crackers. I don't know about you but I've had a hectic day. We can relax with a drink on the back porch."

"Sounds like this side of heaven." Cari headed out of the shop, waving as she left. "Feel free to bring Gifford, I think I can dig up a bone for him." She felt him watching her as she headed home under the sparkling afternoon sun.

Chapter Seven

IN AN ATTEMPT TO FEEL LIKE A GIRL, Cari dashed through the shower when she got home. She stepped out onto the deck in a pretty floral sundress as Ray came up the steps with Gifford beside him. He looked very handsome juggling a tray in one hand and a paper bag in the other.

"Hey!" Ray greeted Cari with a grin.

"Well, aren't you in a good mood! There must be something in the air since it's not even the weekend," she joked. Cari reached out and took the tray artfully arranged with cheese, fruit, prosciutto, sliced vegetables, and crackers.

"You didn't have to do all this, Ray. It's a mini feast but it does look delicious. Please, sit and relax." Cari gestured for Ray to put the bag on the side table.

Shrugging his shoulders, he said, "It wasn't any trouble. There are some nights where I make up something like this for dinner. I happen to be a fan of low fuss, no muss during the summer."

Cari stepped around Gifford and moved to the back door.

"I'm going to grab a frosty mug for your beer and pour myself a glass of wine."

Ray dropped onto a cushioned chair and tapped his leg once. Gifford promptly plopped on the deck, his head coming to rest on his front paws for a snooze.

"All you need are glasses and a corkscrew." Ray pulled the chilled bottle from the bag, holding it up for display. "I think it's what you were drinking the other night."

"That was sweet of you." Cari was touched he remembered which wine she preferred. After a moment's hesitation, she leaned over and pecked his cheek, leaving her scent lingering in the air. Without another word, she slipped into the kitchen.

Cari returned with glassware and small plates. She pointed to a small wicker table where the appetizer tray was sitting. "Would you mind sliding that table between us? I'll start the grill in a bit."

Ray hopped up, happy to rearrange furniture. He glanced around the porch, taking in the fragrant flowers and overstuffed chairs. It was the first time that he could remember the two of them sitting on her porch alone. The ceiling fan made a soft whooshing sound, stirring the air enough for a slight breeze. Cari and Ray settled in and sipped their drinks, both letting out a soft sigh. Sitting in companionable silence, they found simply being together was easy.

Cari's thoughts drifted to Ray's ex-wife, Vanessa. "Can I ask you a question? If I'm getting too personal you don't have to answer."

Ray was surprised. "Sure, ask me anything. If it's too personal I'll say pass and we can skip to another topic." He took a drink of his beer. "I'm ready," he said with a chuckle, "grill me."

"You were married to Vanessa for a long time and you had Jake. It was a surprise to a lot of people when you split up. I mean she left and went to, well I'm not sure where, and you raised Jake. To an observer you looked like a nice committed family unit." She couldn't imagine what had caused Vanessa to take off.

"Well, it's kind of a long story so I won't bore you with all the details but the bottom line was, she fell out of love with me and Jake."

Cari felt she had been knocked over with a feather. "Huh?"

Ray held up his hand. "Vanessa never made an effort to have a relationship with Jake, before or since she left. I often wondered why she wanted to start a family, she hated being pregnant. After he was born she took care of his needs but she never developed a maternal bond with him. She said she wasn't the mothering type. So, after a few years, we stopped talking to each other and we didn't do anything as a family. I found myself spending more time with Jake than with Vanessa. It's very difficult to be in a marriage by yourself. For a while, I tried, or at least I thought I did, but eventually I gave up. I had started my own business, and whenever Jake wasn't in school, I'd take him with me. So, one day we went to do a small job over in Leesville, and when we got home, Vanessa was gone. She had packed her bags and left a note saying she was headed to the west coast. Her parting sentence was 'find a lawyer, file for divorce, and I'm giving you full custody of Jake' and that was that. I never saw her face-to-face again. That was over fifteen years ago."

Ray took a deep breath, so embarrassed with the failure of his marriage he couldn't look at Cari. In a low, deep voice, he continued. "Occasionally, Vanessa would call and talk to Jake. A few times I flew him out to the coast for a visit but the last time he called and asked to come home early and when he got home he said he wasn't going back to California, ever. He felt he was in the way. Vanessa had remarried some poor schmuck with gobs of money. From what Jake has said, it isn't a smooth relationship but if things don't work out, she'll get alimony and move on. After Jake stopped going, she'd call twice a year, at Christmas and his birthday, but that's it. Vanessa hasn't made an effort to see him in the last eight-plus years. As for how I feel about Vanessa, it was like we never were married. I got the best of her when she left, I got Jake." Ray fell into a brooding silence and looked off into the fading sunlight.

Softly, Cari said, "Ray, I'm sorry for you and Jake. No one should ever feel unloved." Her heart broke for the child, abandoned by his mother, and a husband left to pick up the pieces. "So, why didn't you remarry? From personal experience I know how hard it is to raise kids as a single parent." Cari thought about the struggles she had endured. However, her children knew their dad loved them and hadn't willingly left them.

Ray grappled with his answer. He wanted say "because there's no one like you," but pushed that thought away.

"When she first took off, I didn't want anything to do with women. I felt like I had done something wrong, that I was flawed, that I hadn't been a good husband. Maybe Vanessa didn't know how I felt about her, the woman who was my wife, not the woman who was Jake's mom. As time passed, I thought about dating but Jake was going through so much because of Vanessa, and I struggled to be both mother and father to him. I didn't have the energy nor did I want to bring someone around and have him get attached. If it didn't work out, he would have another loss. That would have been too hard for both of us. So, I buried myself in work and spent every free minute with Jake. We played video games, went fishing, built model cars, and hung out. As Jake got older and entered high school I started dating a bit but I found I wasn't meeting many interesting women, so about a year ago I decided to give the Internet dating thing a try. I've had some dates but no one that really makes my heart skip a beat or two."

Cari was drawn to his honesty and love for Jake. "Thank you for telling me. I guess we both share a loss and we have survived." Wishing the awkward moment would pass, Cari stepped over his outstretched legs. "I'd better start the grill otherwise you'll go home without dinner."

"Can I help?" Ray had never shared his pain with anyone and although it had been difficult, he was relieved. Now, Cari knew what had happened.

"Sure, would you grab the salad out of the fridge?" As they moved through the motions of preparing dinner the emotionally charged air began to quiet.

Ray casually moved the conversation to a simpler topic.

"That smells delicious! My mouth's watering. Does cooking come naturally to you or did you go to college for culinary?"

"No formal training, I love to read cookbooks and experiment. You should ask the kids sometime about all the awful dinners they had to eat over the years." Cari placed the platter of fish on the table with gusto. "Dinner is served!"

Their dinner conversation was deliberately casual. Ray and Cari talked about people they knew and what new specialty items she was adding to the shop's menu. As they chatted, Cari's mind kept drifting to their earlier conversation about Ray feeling that he didn't try hard enough in his marriage and that he had failed. She felt he must think that it's easier to blame himself than to blame his ex. It takes two to make a marriage work, and it takes two to break it apart. Vanessa was equally responsible for the failure of their marriage.

As they sat in a satisfied glow Ray couldn't help but wonder about Cari and Ben's marriage. For years, everyone talked about them like they were the perfect couple with a solid marriage. Curiosity got the best of him.

Ray leaned back in his chair, balancing a mug of beer on the arm of the chair.

"Since you asked me questions about my past, can I ask a few?"

"That's fair but the same rules apply. If I don't want to answer, we change the subject." Cari was happy to talk about her life with Ben. Despite the sadness of the last fifteen years, she had had a wonderful marriage. It might help Ray to see that marriage could work with the right person by your side.

"After all these years, why haven't you dated? Don't you want to fall in love and maybe get remarried?" Ray studied her intently.

"Well, that was direct. That's a question most people tap dance around. In the beginning, I was trying to cope with losing Ben and taking care of the kids. You know, we didn't have any warning; one morning he was there and that night a policeman came to our door. Shock doesn't even begin to describe how I felt. I was devastated. There are times when I think it would have been easier for me if he had been sick so I could have been more prepared. When you're young, you don't think your husband's going to die. But as each day passed, it got easier to deal with the daily stuff, what the kids needed, keeping the house running smoothly, and not letting my grief affect the kids. There were many times I would sob in the shower where they couldn't hear me. It's an understatement to say I was depressed. Then I had to pretend I was busy so no one would worry about me. I camped out in a chair and watched a lot of cooking shows. But I needed to do more than watch TV. I needed to keep myself occupied while the kids were in school so I started baking. At first, it was for the kids, but then I branched out and started giving the baked goods away. Baking pulled me out of the depression and it grew from there. People started placing orders and I thought about opening up a shop. Ben did a great job providing for us financially with savings and life insurance but I needed to be able to take care of us. I needed to depend upon myself. I wanted to teach my kids to be strong no matter what life hurls at you. So, I took a deep breath and jumped in with both feet. You know, I found the shop and hired you for renovations and I didn't look back. In the last fourteen years, I can say I haven't felt lonely, but I'm alone. I have a full life but I think the kids are worried I'm going to become the crazy lady who talks to herself. So, Kate and Ellie came up with the idea that I should try dating. Fast forward to today, I signed up and I can't believe what some of these men send in an e-mail!" she said and laughed self-consciously.

Ray was transfixed. He couldn't keep his eyes off her as she talked about her life before and after Ben. She didn't really say much about her relationship with him but she didn't need to, he could tell there was a deep resonating bond and they had had a good life together. He wondered what his life would have been like if he had married someone like Cari instead of his ex. He knew one thing: Life would have been very different if he had found that kind of love.

"So, what advice can you give a girl who has decided to use the Internet to find a date?" Cari decided it was a good point to switch the subject from the past to the present.

Ray was quick to answer. "All kidding aside, a few don'ts: Don't ever give someone your address or home phone number. Use e-mail until you're ready to meet him, and then always in a public place that you drive to yourself. Maybe a diner, or the park on Main Street is always a good choice, lots of people around. Always let someone know where you're going and what time. You're not a child but you don't know who you're meeting and you need to be very careful. If anyone gives you the heebie-geebies, don't go. Don't even respond with a polite 'no, thank you.' Just hit Delete.

"Don't wear anything too revealing or real jewelry. Remember you don't know anything about these guys except what they've told you. First impressions are important, listen to your instincts. If you're uncomfortable, make up an excuse and leave."

Cari struggled not to laugh. "You sound like my dad when I went on my first date." Realizing Ray wasn't joking she nodded solemnly and added, "Thank you, I appreciate the advice."

Ray thought she wasn't taking him seriously. "Some of the women I dated told me exactly where they lived and worked. They gave away their personal information too freely. If I wasn't a decent guy they could have been in for a nasty surprise. I don't want you to make the same mistakes and potentially get into trouble. If you ever get in over your head, keep my number on speed dial and I'll come and get you. No questions asked."

In a flash Cari saw him as her knight, speeding to her rescue. Tucking the image away, she changed the subject. "How about some dessert and then we can talk about our joint project? I have berries, whipped cream, and sponge cake."

Cari placed the dirty dishes on a tray and Ray carried it inside. They returned to the back porch with dessert plates in hand. Cari saw Ray glance a look at his watch.

Ray didn't seem to be in a hurry to leave so Cari broached a topic that had been troubling her. "You aren't neglecting your other jobs for this one are you?"

"No, it's worked out just fine. Jake and I needed inside jobs so we would have a project on rainy days, and I have some jobs lined up for more renovation work and furniture. I don't think we'll get another mild winter like we had last year. The Farmer's Almanac is calling for heavy snow this year. You know, I had a thought. What do you think about installing a small pellet or wood stove. With the additional windows it would make the room feel cozy and provide extra heat."

Her interest piqued, Cari said, "Hmm, I never thought of a stove but I do like a fire, and we have a fireplace in the living room. I don't use it often, except for holidays or if the family is over for Sunday dinner. Do we need a chimney? And will it delay completion of the room?"

"If you go with the pellet stove I can tell you they're easy to install and you don't need a brick chimney. We can do the same with the wood stove and get approved piping to vent it. I think before you decide you should stop in at A & E Fireplace and see what you like. You need to think about hauling bags of pellets, or if wood is more to your liking. They both will have flames so it's really a matter of which one works best for you."

"I don't have to think about it. I can imagine a wood stove tucked into the room and a cast iron pot simmering with stew or thick soup cooking on a cold winter day. Ray, you are just full of great ideas."

"Slow down." Ray chuckled. "You don't have to decide

today. I'd be happy to go with you and oversee the installation. If you don't have any plans after work tomorrow, we can decide the best place for it and take measurements. We should add brick or a stone facade around it for safety and to meet the building codes."

"Excellent!" Cari said, clapping her hands in excitement. "I don't remember the last time I had so much fun spending money. Ray, this project is turning out to be a blast and it's going to be the best sunroom ever!"

"Well, I wouldn't go that far but I'll certainly do my best."

Chapter Eight

THE DAYS PASSED QUICKLY, and late summer turned into a warm fall. One afternoon, Cari left the shop early to see what she might have in her closet that would be suitable for the following day. It was to be her first date with someone who had been messaging her from the dating site. After several e-mails back and forth as well as a short phone call, she accepted Al's invitation. He was the best choice out of the group that had contacted her. Kate and Ellie would be over after dinner, they wanted final approval on her outfit Cari wanted to look nice but didn't want it to look like she was trying too hard. Thank heavens it was just coffee.

Cari wandered around her backyard, admiring the new French doors and the fancy trim boards. She couldn't wait until her house was whole again. She was grateful Ray had taken her along when he chose the windows. She had bought oak boards to build a shelf. Another time they had gone to check out pellet and wood stoves. In the end, she ordered an energy-efficient wood stove. It was fun taking day trips with Ray and being involved in each aspect of the renovation.

As she wandered absentmindedly through the garden, daydreaming about a hearty stew simmering on the wood stove and Ray enjoying it with her, a flash of color caught her attention. There was a woman walking in Ray's backyard and trying to get in the back door. Who on earth was prowling around, she wondered. Curiosity overruled common sense and she crossed to the property edge. "Hello? Can I help you?" she called out.

A tall, devastatingly beautiful blonde turned to her and snarled, "I'm looking for my husband."

Caught off guard, Cari asked, "Are you sure you have the right house? The gentleman who lives here isn't married."

"My husband is Ray Davis and I know he owns this house. Do you usually see people wandering around trying to get into someone's house in broad daylight? What are you, stupid or just nosy?" The blonde turned on her heel and strode off around to the front of the house.

What the heck was going on here? Ray had been divorced for years . . . although this woman looked vaguely familiar. Cari watched as the woman stormed off toward the front of the house after dropping that bombshell. Cari followed her. Parked in the driveway was a late model BMW convertible with California plates. Something fishy was going on and Cari had no intention of letting her loiter. There was no telling what she'd do.

"Excuse me, you should ask permission to be on someone's property. Since Ray isn't home, don't you think you should leave?" the woman snapped.

"Allow me to introduce myself. I'm Cari McKenna, and you are?" Cari waited as the blonde looked her up and down.

"I am Vanessa Davis. What is your relationship with my husband?"

Mildly annoyed, Cari ignored the question. "I'm sorry. It was my understanding that you and Ray have been divorced for years."

"Oh, that's a technicality. I'm back and things are going to be better than ever."

Vanessa carefully scrutinized Cari. She didn't think this rinky-dink little town had any women that were attractive but this one standing in front of her wasn't what she had expected. Other than being short, her hair was a lovely mix of black with auburn highlights, her green eyes shimmered like emeralds, her flawless skin had a hint of natural color in her cheeks, and she had a shapely figure. She might be the competition. Vanessa was sure her ex-husband had noticed his neighbor and wondered what was going on between them. It was a little too cozy for Vanessa's taste and Cari had butted in when she was trying to get in the house.

"Ray isn't expecting me. I decided to surprise him." Vanessa thought no one needed to know what she was hiding; it was no one's business but hers.

"Oh, I'm sure he's going to be surprised." Cari's voice was laced with sarcasm. She wasn't buying what Vanessa was selling. This wasn't about rekindling the marriage. So, what was the real motivation for the sudden appearance?

Vanessa didn't miss Cari's tone. She was banking on Ray being grateful that she would see Jake while in town. Maybe since he hadn't remarried and wasn't living with someone he had never gotten over her. After all, who could replace her?

Cari didn't miss Vanessa's smug look. Under her breath she muttered, "Lady, you're in for a rude awakening." Then, louder, she added, "Based on my conversation with Ray, he isn't in love with you, and he hates what you did to Jake."

Vanessa glared at Cari. "Well, Ray should be home soon and if you don't want to witness the happy reunion maybe you should find your way back to where you came from. I don't need for you to keep me company."

Cari couldn't believe the audacity of this woman. Did she really think Ray was going to welcome her with open arms? "You're right. I don't want to be around when Ray finds you camped out on his doorstep. Hopefully it won't rain while you're waiting." Cari looked up. "There's a storm brewing."

"You don't need to worry about me. I'm sure I'll find my key and be snug and dry long before the rain starts."

Cari gave Vanessa one final look and turned to walk away. "Don't count on it."

Cari walked up her back steps. The sky opened up and a cold driving rain came down in sheets. Cari glanced back over her shoulder to see Vanessa standing in the middle of the driveway, frantically digging through her shoulder bag. Satisfied, Cari went inside where it was warm and dry.

In a desperate attempt to protect her hair, Vanessa pulled her bag up over her head and dashed to the car. As she pulled on the door handle, her bag slipped, leaving her in the drenching rain. Vanessa shouted at the stuck door, "Great!" Continuing to pull on the door she grumbled, "When Ray sees me I'll look like something the dog dragged in. Not the best way to greet your ex-husband especially when I intend to wrap him around my finger." She gave the door a hard yank and it flew open, allowing her to dive inside.

Ray drove up his road and noticed a BMW in his driveway. "Gif, who the heck is at the house?" Upon closer scrutiny, he saw California plates. "This can't be good."

Sitting behind the foggy windshield, Vanessa wiped the condensation off just in time to see a dark blue truck park in front of the garage. She positioned the car for a good view of the road so she could have a few moments to pull herself together before she got out of the car. Taking a deep breath and running a hand over her limp hair, she opened the car door and gracefully slid out. Her eyes were locked on Ray as she glided over, stopping within inches of his lean body.

Ray's day went downhill, fast. He recognized her the moment she stepped out of the car. Her movements were catlike, ready to spring on an unsuspecting mouse, or at least that was Ray's impression as the distance between them was reduced.

"Vanessa, I see you remember where I live. What are you doing here?" Ray's voice was filled with contempt. "It's been a long time, what, fifteen years or so?"

Vanessa planted a kiss on his mouth. "Now that isn't any way to talk to your wife, is it? And do I need to remind you, this is our house."

Gifford was standing next to Ray, grumbling a warning low in his throat. Ray placed a reassuring hand on his head.

"Ex-wife, former home, I bought you out, remember?" Ray glanced in the direction of Cari's house.

Vanessa's eyes followed his gaze and her radar went up.

"Don't worry, your neighbor has already poked her snoopy nose in our business. In fact, she left right before the rain started." This might be a slight complication but she was sure she could handle Cari. Just like she was confident in her ability to manipulate Ray.

"What do you want, Vanessa?" he growled. "I'm sure you're not pining for your son. You haven't bothered with him in years. You didn't even attempt to come to his wedding. Not like you've ever had much interest in him. If you had something to talk about, you should have called."

"That's not fair. I knew that I wasn't being a good wife or mother to you two so I left. Looking back, maybe I should have talked to you about how I was feeling. I'm not the person that you remember—I've changed!" she wailed.

"Fair? Let's talk about fair. One morning I had a wife. Jake had a mother. I went to work so you could have the lifestyle you wanted and when I get home, what's waiting for me? A note. That's it. You couldn't bother tell us in person. You didn't care enough to say good-bye to your son. So, you think I'm not being fair? That's rich." Ray turned on his heel and strode toward the side door, Gifford at his side.

Vanessa ran after him, struggling to keep up. "Wait, let me explain! I'm begging you." He stopped short and she ran into him, knocking her back and slightly off balance.

Gifford bared his teeth and growled, causing Vanessa to stop in her tracks.

"Easy boy." Ray held his collar.

"Vanessa, it's time for you to leave. Go home. You're not wanted or welcome here." Ray turned and looked her directly in the eye. His hard stare held firm. There was no softening him.

"May I use your bathroom before I go? It's been a long drive and I've been waiting for you for hours. I could use to freshen up a bit. Please?" Vanessa's big blue eyes caught his. She prayed the look would still work its magic.

"All right," he grumbled, "but don't get comfortable, this hasn't been your home in years. And don't track mud all through the kitchen. In case you forgot there's a bathroom right inside the back entrance."

Vanessa took the small victory. "I remember, Ray. I remember lots of things." She hoped she could get him riled up with a suggestive promise of something that stirred a man's insides.

Ray grumbled. "Vanessa, that's ancient history and it won't work anymore." He opened the back door and let her step in ahead of him. He planned to keep a close eye on her and get her out as quickly as possible.

Vanessa peeked into the kitchen as she made her way to the powder room. The house sparkled, inside and out. She didn't remember the house being this nice when she lived here. She peered into the mirror and scrutinized her appearance. Her makeup was smeared, and her hair was a tangled mess. No wonder he wasn't thrilled to see me, she thought. What did she expect? Show up unannounced and looking like a drowned rat. Well she would take a few minutes to fix her face and hair. Maybe then things would smooth out between them.

Ray was staring out the window deep in thought when Vanessa made her grand appearance. "What took you so long, were you rifling through my medicine cabinet?"

"Ray, I'm sorry." Vanessa's first reaction was to snap, but she changed her tactics midretort.

"For what, walking out or that you're in my house?" Ray was skeptical of every word, there was too much history.

"I'm sorry I hurt you and Jake. You're my family and I didn't know how to tell you I was unhappy. You thrived on small-town life and I hated it. I didn't want to become a country mouse. I wanted us to travel, see the world. All you needed was outside the front door. I needed things that I knew you'd never be able to give me. I didn't want to just scrape by, worrying about how we'd send Jake to college. I thought if I left I would be able to help give Jake the future he deserved—college and a life that went beyond Loudon."

Vanessa looked down at the floor, letting her apology hang in the air.

"Vanessa, you walked away because we didn't have money?" Ray couldn't believe his ears. "We always had enough money, we were healthy, a good roof over our heads, plenty of food, and a vacation every year. That wasn't enough for you? Many people get by on much less than what we had."

Vanessa quickly realized she needed to tread lightly. "It wasn't just about money. It was about this hole in the wall town. I worried about people taking advantage of you. You always helped others but no one ever offered to help us. I thought they would bleed us dry and I couldn't stand by and watch. At first, I didn't want to uproot Jake in the middle of the school year. By leaving Jake with you, I did what was best for him. Then, when I was settled, he didn't want to come out to California. He resented me for leaving him and you didn't help matters. You didn't make him see me. So I did the only thing I could, I stayed away."

Ray was stunned. She actually believed her version of the truth. "Vanessa, I help people because it makes me feel good. It's not about what someone can do for me. These people, you say were taking advantage of me, they are my friends and neighbors. If someone needed help, then I'm proud to say that I was there for them. If you ever bothered to get to know any of them, you would have found our neighbors were good people. And 'these' people stood by me and Jake when we needed support."

Vanessa sensed a losing battle so she diverted to the present. "Speaking of neighbors, what's going on between you and that woman?" Vanessa jerked her head in the direction of Cari's house.

"I don't have to explain anything to you and I don't appreciate your tone. My personal life is off limits to you."

"It seems a little strange that she would come waltzing over here to check me out when you're not home. I don't remember her from when we were married." She was still trying to discover what their relationship was. Her plan might fizzle before it got started.

"That's what good neighbors do; we watch out for each other including when we're not home. If Cari didn't recognize you, I'm not surprised since you never bothered to become friends with her or anyone else in town. But again, I don't have to explain my relationships to you. You lost that privilege when you took off."

Ray opened up the back door, took her arm, and firmly steered her out to the car. "I think our reunion is over." He opened the car door and waited for her to get in.

Vanessa slid behind the wheel and pleaded, "Ray, don't make me leave, I need your help. Please?"

"NO! Do what you do best, Vanessa. Leave." Ray slammed the door.

Vanessa fumed as she jerked the car into reverse. How dare he dismiss her as if she were a mere acquaintance! She peeled out of the driveway, kicking up stones in her wake. "This isn't over, Ray, we're just getting started." She snarled at his reflection in the rearview mirror.

Vanessa glanced in the side mirror just before the final turn on Main Street. Ray was standing at the end of the driveway, watching the car. She'd go for now, but she'd be back. She'd find a cheap hotel room in Leesville and wait. For now, she needed to keep a low profile.

Drained from the encounter with Vanessa, Ray wanted to explain to Cari. But he had no idea what he could tell her. With heavy thoughts, he tromped through the wet grass. As he reached her back door, the sun burst from the dark clouds. He rapped sharply on the door, hoping she was home.

Cari watched Ray slowly make his way to her house. Relieved to see he was alone, she pulled open the door even before he could knock.

"Come on in. You look like you could use a friend." Cari's crooked smile warmed his heart. The black cloud that hovered slid away.

"How do you do that?" he asked her.

"Do what?" Cari handed him a glass of iced tea and gestured for him to have a seat on the back porch.

"You always seem to know just what I need, and you make my insides smile. Forget what I just said, it didn't make any sense." Ray shrugged his shoulders and dropped into what had become his favorite chair. If he paid attention, it would have surprised him to find they had established a routine when they were together.

Cari secretly smiled. "Well, you know I'm Irish and just a little fey. So sometimes I just know what I know."

"Ah, now it makes sense." He chuckled. "I heard you met my ex. Do you mind telling me what happened? I have a feeling she spun her story to give you the impression I'd welcome her with open arms."

"When I got home from work I saw a woman jiggling the doorknob on your back door. I could hear her yelling. The words that were coming out of her mouth would make a sailor blush. I watched her for a few more minutes and it appeared she was searching for a key, picking up the flowerpots on the steps. I was afraid she'd break a window, so I went over. I figured if you had been expecting someone you would have been there waiting for them or told me in case you got hung up."

"Yeah, I would have said something," he agreed.

"As I got closer I realized that she knew whose house it was. I called out to her. I guess that caught her off guard. She snapped my head off, telling me she was your wife and then proceeded to ask me if I was stupid. I took the comment in stride, knowing I interrupted her attempt to break-in. We talked for a few more minutes and I thought it might rain so I came back over. It started to rain and Vanessa got drenched, which I'm sure did nothing to improve her mood." Cari laughed.

"You think this is funny?" Ray was ticked off.

"Hold on for a minute, Ray. If you could have seen her face when it started pouring, she was soaked in seconds. She held her handbag over her hair, thinking that somehow it was going to protect it. It really was too funny." Cari smirked.

The mental picture of a perfectly coiffed Vanessa formed and he started laughing, too. "I guess she wanted to make a grand entrance. Maybe she should have packed an umbrella. Cari, thanks, I'm glad I came over. Your story put everything into perspective."

Cari turned serious. "Ray, you need to give Jake a heads-up that his mother's lurking around, and the sooner the better. He has unresolved feelings toward Vanessa. She could use that to hurt both of you."

Ray sat in the chair, absentmindedly running his finger and thumb over his mustache and down to his chin. "I don't have my cell with me but I'll call Jake as soon as I get home. Do you really think she'll go see him?"

"If she is saying that you're her husband, then she'll see Jake. Don't underestimate her. I can't put my finger on it but whatever brought her to town definitely isn't going to be good for anyone."

Ray felt an icy cold finger run down his spine. He didn't say anything but he agreed with Cari.

"Don't worry, Ray. I'll keep my eyes open and if I see her around the house I'll call you or Jake. Our sons are like brothers. Vanessa will answer to me if she tries to hurt either you or Jake," Cari vowed.

Chapter Nine

RAY KNEW HOW JAKE WOULD REACT TO THE NEWS that Vanessa was in town, and he didn't delay in calling him.

Jake answered his phone on the second ring. "Dad, why is she in town? Oh no, do you think she knows where we live?" Jake's immediate thought was keeping his mother away from his wife.

"Son, you know it's only a matter of time before she tracks you and Sara down. You don't have a choice. You have to tell Sara before Vanessa finds her."

"You're right. I never expected to see her again. I'll talk to you in the morning. G'night, Dad."

Exhausted, Ray flopped in his recliner and propped his feet up. What a day. All he wanted to do when he got home was steal a couple of minutes with Cari. He was curious if she had any luck with the dating site. Restless, Ray stood up, frustrated and irritated with the day's events. If he had any guts, he'd ask Cari out on a date and show her how much fun it could be. He had carried a torch for Cari probably longer than he'd admit even to himself. He had dated casually the last few years but never long enough for anyone to get attached. He compared every woman to Cari. Where this woman was concerned, his legs were stuck in cement. He needed to get up the gumption to ask her out or settle for friendship and move on.

He crossed to the kitchen and peered in the refrigerator. Scanning the contents, he didn't see anything that was appealing. "Pizza it is," he said out loud. He grabbed his keys, but half way out the door changed his mind, turned around, took the phone off the hook, and punched in a series of numbers.

Breathless, Cari said, "Hello?"

"Hey, did you make dinner yet? I'm going for pizza and wondered if you wanted to come along?"

"Um, sure. What time are you going?" She wasn't about to tell Ray she had been cleaning the kitchen and looked like a mess.

"How does five minutes sound? I'm starving." He was anxious to see her.

"Can you make it ten? I'd like to feel human if we're going to be eating in public and I don't think you'll die of starvation before we get there." She laughed.

"I'll swing by and pick you up." Ray hung up without saying good-bye.

Cari looked at the receiver for a second. With no time to waste, she dashed up the stairs, pulling her shirt off before she got to her bedroom. She rifled through the closet and grabbed a fresh yellow T-shirt, ran a brush through her hair, and applied a swish of mascara. A quick look in the mirror confirmed she was presentable. She heard a light honk. Peeking out the window, she saw Ray striding up the walk.

Ray rapped sharply on the front door. Frowning, he thought a friend wouldn't knock on another friend's front door to go out to dinner. Before he could think about what he was going to say, Cari flung open the door flashing him a megawatt smile.

"This is a great idea. I haven't been out for pizza in ages."

"I thought I would run out and pick up something to bring home. By the time I get home, the pizza will be cold. And then I thought you might like a slice. So here I am." Ray shrugged.

The sharp edginess Ray had been feeling melted away as soon as he laid eyes on her. Cari could soothe him with a smile or light touch on the arm. In that instant, Ray decided he would find a way to convince her to become a significant part of his life.

Cari grabbed her fleece and handbag from the side chair. She and Ray walked in silence to the truck.

"Thanks for coming with me tonight. It gets old, don't you think, eating alone?" Ray held the door open at the same time he glanced down, embarrassed to see papers covering the front seat. He scooped them up and dropped them in the back. Sheepishly he said, "My mobile filing system. I guess I should have cleaned up the truck before coming over."

"That's okay. You should see the inside of my car some days. I dump out my bag on the seat when I've been digging around and can't find something." Cari thought it was sweet he was flustered.

Lightening up the mood, he said, "You? I doubt you've ever had a day where things weren't exactly where they should be. You are extremely organized."

"I have my moments, just like everyone else," she assured him. Cari fished her phone out of her handbag. "What time do you think we'll be back? The girls are stopping by later and I should let them know I'll be out for a while." She hoped the girls wouldn't mind the slight change of plans.

"An hour or so. We're early so I think we'll miss the dinner rush." Secretly pleased to have an hour with her, he was going to savor every minute.

"Just give me a minute and I'll text them."

Ray watched Cari's hair fall across her face. Her brows wrinkled together as she concentrated on the short message. He had to remind himself to breathe as he watched her.

Cari typed in a few words, flipped the cover shut, and slipped the phone back into her bag. "All set! Now let's get serious for a minute. What kind of pizza should we order? I love everything except pineapple."

He glanced at her out of the corner of his eye, keeping track of the road in front of them. It didn't matter to him, she could ask for chocolate chips and he'd happily eat them.

"I can eat anything, lady's choice. But think fast, we're here."

Ray pulled up in front of Slices Pizzeria. The large windows revealed most of the tables were empty.

"Look, there's Grace and Charlie." Cari pointed to a table where her best friends were having dinner.

Ray held the door for Cari as they walked in. She waved to Grace and Charlie. "Hello, you two!" Cari silently prayed Grace wouldn't ask them to share a table.

Suppressing her surprise, Grace said, "Hey yourself, what brings you out tonight?" Grace was dying to know what was going on but she'd have to wait until later to pump Cari for information.

"Ray was coming out for pizza and asked me if I wanted to tag along. So here we are." Cari grinned at her friends and suddenly felt self-conscious. "We need to get going. The girls are coming over later. I'll call you tomorrow?"

Grace nodded and Charlie shook Ray's hand. "Good to see you. Ray. You guys enjoy your dinner."

Ray and Cari moved away from the table toward a booth on the other side of the room.

Grace and Charlie looked at each other with eyebrows raised. "What do you make of this?" Grace asked in a hushed tone and continued, "Do you think this is a good idea? I don't want Cari to be alone, but I'm not sure if Ray is the right guy for her."

Charlie's eyes followed Grace's gaze. He and Ben had been best friends and he knew that Cari hadn't dated anyone since Ben had died. "What do you mean 'is this a good idea'? Don't you think you're being overprotective of Cari? She is a grown woman and we have known Ray for years. You've always liked him. Besides, Kate has been watching them tap dance around each other for a couple of years and she's pretty sure they have feelings for each other but they're too blind to see it. I say we support 'this,' whatever it is."

Out of the corner of her eye, Grace continued to watch them. "I know Cari and Ray have been out for pizza before but it was always with the kids. This is definitely a change in the status quo. I wonder if the girls know who their mother is having dinner with tonight?" she mused.

Ray and Cari settled into a corner booth. Even though most of the tables were empty, they took a table toward the back so they could talk over frosty mugs of beer, relax and wait for the pizza.

"So, about today," Ray began. "I'm sorry about Vanessa." He paused. "I wasn't thinking straight. I appreciate that you prompted me to call Jake. He shouldn't be blindsided by his mother."

The waitress delivered their pizza and salad. Cari slid a slice topped with hot gooey cheese and sausage onto each of their plates.

Cari passed a plate to Ray and placed her hand on top of his. "Ray, you would have done the same for me. I admit I was taken aback when she referred to herself as your wife and then announced she was going to smooth things over with you and Jake. It sounds like she wants you back."

"That will be the day hell freezes over," Ray said sarcastically. "After some of the things she said today about our life together I can't believe she would think that I'd ever take her back. She's insane." Ray reluctantly removed his hand from underneath Cari's and picked up his slice.

"Why do you suppose she's here? I can't understand what would motivate her to come back. From what you have said, she hated it here."

"I honestly don't know. She's a selfish person and whatever the reason, you better believe, somehow, she'll come out smelling like a rose."

Cari mulled over the conversation she had had with Vanessa. It was obvious Vanessa was up to no good. They all needed to be on guard until they knew why.

"Well, enough talk of Vanessa. What are your plans for the rest of the weekend?" Ray was hoping to spend some more time with her.

Cari hesitated. "Not much. Some gardening, housework, overall pretty low key." Offhandedly, she continued, "I have a coffee date tomorrow morning. I'm meeting him in Everett at ten."

"Is he someone you met online?" Ray's mood turned sour as the green monster reared his ugly head in the pit of Ray's gut.

"Yes, he e-mailed me a couple of weeks ago and we have been e-mailing every couple of days, and we also talked on the phone. He asked me if I'd like to meet him for coffee. So I agreed to meet him." Cari was uncomfortable telling Ray.

Ray's heart sank, but he masked his feelings. "That's great, Cari!" He wished he could be the guy waiting for her at the coffee shop and not some stranger. "When you get back, stop over. We can dissect it. First dates can be nerve-racking."

Relief washed over her. "Thanks for the support. I'm so nervous, and it'll be good to get a man's perspective."

After they finished dinner Cari insisted they split the check. Ray reluctantly agreed and they strolled to his truck for the short drive home. When he dropped her off Ray said, "Remember, come by tomorrow for coffee."

"Thanks for dinner. I'll see you at some point." Cari waved and walked up to the brightly lit house. As usual, the girls were keeping the electric company in business. She smiled to herself. It was nice to have someone waiting for her to come home.

The aroma of popcorn greeted her at the front door. Quiet laughter drifted to her from the back of the house. Dropping her bag and coat on the table, she walked through the semidarkness in search of her girls. "Sounds like you started the party without me."

Kate and Ellie were sitting on the floor, laughing so hard tears were rolling down their cheeks. It was good to see them having fun together. She had spent many nights reassuring Ellie to be patient, that someday she and Kate would be best friends. When Ellie wanted to play dolls, Kate said she was too old. When Ellie had outgrown dolls, Kate had graduated to boys and Ellie thought they were gross. Then Kate went to college and left her. How Ellie had cried, heartbroken. Shane moved into an apartment that same spring, which left Ellie with her mom for companionship. The house hadn't been the same since the twins moved out.

Ellie's voice broke into her brief journey down memory lane. "Earth to Mom. How did you end up having dinner with Ray?"

Cari said nonchalantly, "He asked and I said yes."

Kate and Ellie stole a look between each other. "Okay, is that the story you're sticking with?" said Kate, and they both giggled in unison. "Of course, we know it's nothing more than dinner between old friends."

"I didn't say we were old so stop putting words in my mouth. Let's get some iced tea and go pick out what I'm going to wear tomorrow for my date. If you put a wiggle on it, I'll tell you about Ray's ex-wife showing up today. She's a beautiful nightmare."

"This is shaping up to be an interesting night and we're just getting started," Kate mused.

Cari led the way upstairs to her room with the girls close behind her. She turned on the bedside lamp resting on the nightstand, bathing her bedroom in soft light. Cari crossed the room and flipped the switch, illuminating her dressing area in a bright warm glow. Her bedroom was soft tones of purple, cream, and pale green. The walls were papered in a hydrangea pattern and creamy white wainscoting set it off. An overstuffed chair and ottoman sat adjacent to the over-size windows that were draped in floor-length sheer curtains. Cari liked to wake to the sun sliding over the wide, polished pine floorboards. In the summer, the windows were open wide allowing a soft breeze to carry the fresh scent of flowers inside. Leftover from another era, a brick fireplace took up one wall, the mantle covered with cherished family photos.

Ellie paused on the threshold; this was her favorite room in the house. "Kate, remember the hours we spent in this room? We would climb up on Mom's bed and snuggle in, and she'd tell us stories. We were mesmerized by the princess stories. And on cold winter afternoons, we'd have a fire and roast marshmallows. Shane would come in for the marshmallows but he said story time was for girls."

"Ah, but did you know he would sit outside the door, just out of sight, listening? On a rare occasion, he would drift in, pretending he was checking on everyone, always the man of the house. He started that after your dad died." Cari smiled at the sweet memory.

"No story time tonight, El," Kate teased, "We need to help Mom get ready for her big date. It's been a long time since Mom's gone out with a guy without a bunch of kids hanging around." Deliberately, Kate threw in the reference to pizza nights between the Davises and McKennas.

"Girls, it's not that big of a deal, it's just coffee." Exasperated, Cari watched as Kate dug through her jewelry and Ellie rifled through her closet.

Kate had laid out a pair of jeans, black cowboy boots and a long necklace but Ellie had yet to find the right blouse. "Mom, don't you have anything that has some color or pattern? Everything you have that is sort of dressy, is basic black. I should have checked your closet before tonight. We should have gone shopping at the mall or at least in town. Joyful Threads—you know that new place on Main Street?—has some cute clothes. Katie, have you looked in here?" Ellie said. "It's a fashion crime. Some of this stuff desperately needs to go to the thrift store, if they'll even take it."

Kate crossed to the closet and nudged her sister aside. "Let me see. There has to be something that will work. Unfortunately, my clothes won't fit because I'm taller, and

Pixie, well frankly, I don't know anyone who can borrow your clothes."

Ellie didn't take offense. She liked being petite, it helped her stand out from the long shadows her sister and brother cast.

"El, check Mom's scarf drawer. Last year I gave her one that will dress up the black silk blouse. It looks like a Monet painting."

"Found it!" Ellie cried victoriously, holding up a silk scarf with a riot of soft colors. It was the perfect accent to the shirt that Kate held up.

Cari watched as her room became a jumbled mess. It would take twice as long to make it neat as it was taking the girls to create a tornado of clothes and accessories.

"What do you think, Mom? It's comfortable, relaxed, and you won't be overdressed." Kate and Ellie were pleased with the outfit they pulled together.

"The blouse is one of my favorites and I had never thought to pair it with the scarf. It's a great look and perfect with jeans. I have one question: What about a jacket? It's supposed to be chilly tomorrow." The girls looked at each other, mentally running through her jackets.

"Mom, where's the suede blazer that you bought eons ago? It's classic." Kate pulled out a pair of hoop earrings and dropped them into Cari's hand. "This outfit will knock his socks off unless he's blind. You're going to look amazing."

Ellie bobbed her head in agreement.

Cari looked at her reflection in the mirror. Looking back was a nervous seventeen-year-old getting ready for her first date. She certainly didn't feel like a mother of three adults. Panic started to set in. "I must be crazy. What am I doing, meeting a complete stranger for coffee? What if we have nothing to talk about? I've changed my mind and I'm going to send him an e-mail and cancel."

Cari's eyes caught her girls looking at her reflection in the mirror.

"No, you're not canceling. If you have nothing to talk about, you drink your coffee, drop a couple of dollars on the table, and leave. If it's really uncomfortable, leave. Either way, you'll be fine." Kate attempted to soothe her nerves.

"Are you sure it's okay that I'm going to date?" Doubt was written across Cari's face.

"Oh, Mom," said Kate as the girls sandwiched Cari between them. "You deserve to have a great guy in your life and be happy. You've been alone a long time, and Daddy wouldn't want you to live this way. This is a good first step to living a full, happy life with someone."

Ellie kissed her mom on the cheek. "Mommy, this is a good thing." At times, she felt guilty, she was out with her friends, and her mom was home alone. She'd feel better knowing Cari was out kicking up her heels, too.

Cari hugged her girls, walked to the chair, and laid the outfit over the back.

Kate was dying of curiosity. "So, tell us about dinner with Ray, and what's the story with his ex? She's in town?"

Cari relayed all the details about Vanessa showing up and proclaiming to be his wife and then correcting herself to say they'd be getting back together. "She was annoyed that I came over and got in what she said was personal between her and Ray. The best part was when the sky opened up and a downpour drenched her. She ended up looking like a drowned blond rat. I sat on the back porch laughing as she stood there yelling at the rain."

Amused, Kate asked, "Mom? Didn't you ask her to look up at the sky?"

Cari smirked. "Well, I thought about it but she was too busy telling me to leave. Whoever said there isn't poetic justice!" The three women giggled long into the evening.

Chapter Ten

CARI PEERED INTO THE BATHROOM MIRROR. The bags under her eyes told the tale of a sleepless night. Studying her face, she wondered if Al would take one look and decide she was an old hag.

Her thoughts wandered as she went through her morning routine. When had dating become so complicated and nerve-racking? It used to be easy. In college, you met a guy who was friends with a friend, you asked around about him, let him know you were interested, and he asked you out. You'd date for a while, see if it was a good fit, and if not, no big deal. If you clicked, life was good. Now with everyone married, living with someone, or happily single the alternative is the Internet. Meeting people was a new realm of odd. You create a profile, checking off what you like and don't like. Someone will see it and maybe they'll e-mail you, or if you see someone you like, you e-mail him or her. Then you take a chance and meet.

Talking to the woman in the mirror she announced, "I'm not thrilled with this idea, but I guess Internet dating is the way to go, and living in a small town it gives me a bigger pond to go fishing in."

Cari ate a leisurely breakfast, lingering over coffee. She enjoyed the view from the nook window, watching the squirrels scamper back and forth over the back lawn, gathering nuts for winter. She noticed the leaves littered the yard and mentally added raking to her afternoon to-do list. It would be great to get some fresh air and potentially she could bump into Ray. She glanced at the wall clock. Time to go.

Cari walked into the diner ten minutes early and took a table in the center that faced the door. A waitress came over with a coffee pot in hand. "Hi, do you know what you'd like?" she said as she poured steaming coffee into a mug.

"Thank you. I'm waiting for someone. He should be here soon."

The waitress nodded and moved to the next table.

Cari stirred cream and sugar into her cup. She brought a book so she could blend in with the crowd. It was propped open but she wasn't able to concentrate. After waiting twenty minutes, she pulled out her cell. No messages. She waited another five minutes and called Grace.

"Hi, Grace, it's me." Before Grace could say a word, Cari blurted out, "How long do I wait for this guy to show up?" Cari felt foolish and embarrassed.

"He's not there yet?" Grace sounded ticked, suspecting she had been stood up. "Did he call?"

"No, and no one that remotely looks like him has come into the diner. So, how long do I wait?" Cari's self-confidence had plummeted. Dejected, she said, "Maybe he took one look at me through the window and didn't want to bother coming in."

"Girlfriend, get your stuff and leave. You've been waiting long enough for this jerk and you're done!" Grace's anger seeped through the phone.

"Okay, I'll call you later, and Grace, thanks for being there when I needed you." Cari left a couple of dollars on the table and went out to the sidewalk just as a guy who looked like Al came sauntering up.

"Hey, Cari?" Thrusting out his hand, he clamped down on hers like a vise and shook vigorously.

"Yes. Al? I'm sorry I must have gotten the time mixed up. I thought we were meeting at ten."

"Sorry 'bout that. Just lost track of time and, well, you know how it goes. Do you still want to have a cup of joe?"

Irritated, Cari glanced at her watch. "Well, I'm meeting someone in a while so maybe another time."

Al shrugged his shoulders. "Sure, no prob. I'll send you

an e-mail, and we can set something up. See ya later." He walked off humming off-key.

Stunned at the lack of manners, she fumed to herself, "This is what dating is all about these days? Not bothering to show up on time. I certainly hope this isn't a recurring theme."

Cari slowly drove up her street and caught a glimpse of Ray working in his yard. She pulled over and rolled her window down.

Leaning on his rake, he glanced at his watch. Surprised to see her, he said, "I didn't expect to see you home so soon. What happened?"

"Hi. Well, that was a waste of time," she said and proceeded to give Ray the highlights of her morning. "He was about twenty-five minutes late and showed up as I was walking to my car. He introduced himself, saying he lost track of time and didn't bother to apologize. He asked if we could do it another time, but I don't think so." Cari's green eyes flashed. It was a look he didn't see often. The drive home hadn't done anything to calm her down.

"I've got a pot of coffee on. Would you like to have a cup with me?"

"That sounds nice. Let me pull my car off the road."

Cari parked and crossed to where he waited for her. "This is a switch, you making me coffee?" Laughing, they strolled around to the back deck. Cari sat down in the warm autumn sun and admired his gardens.

"Cream and sugar?" he called out from the kitchen. Ray had watched her make a cup for years so he knew exactly how she liked it.

"Yes, please." Cari carefully took the hot mug and brought the steaming brew to her lips, taking a tiny sip. "It's perfect, just the right amount of cream and sugar." Her eyes lit up. "It is a beautiful day and much too nice to be sitting inside a diner. This is so much better. Seriously, Ray, how do you do it? Put yourself out there, trying to meet people?

Is today what I should expect from other first dates?"

"Cari, when you meet someone think of them as a new friend and see where it goes. If you don't like the guy, it won't be a big deal. We've been friends for years, and I think you're a terrific girl. When you find the right guy, you'll know it, and he'll be a lucky guy."

Cari blushed. "Ray, you're sweet. Maybe you could clone yourself and that way I'll have a great guy." Cari felt the pit of her stomach flip over. "I better get going. I interrupted your work and I have a lot to get done, too." She wanted to call the girls and tell them her date had been a failure. So much for choosing the perfect outfit, she thought ruefully.

Ray seemed to read her mind. "Cari, you look really pretty today. That jerk probably took one look at you and knew you were out of his league."

Slightly embarrassed, Cari diverted the conversation. "You want a laugh? Al said he was five-foot-ten, well, it was on the minus side. He's my height. It makes me wonder what else he lied about."

"Sounds like you might have dodged a bullet, my friend. Lying about your height? That's something hard to explain later. Well, I guess he could have said it was a typo."

Feeling better about things, Cari finished her coffee. "I'm going home, calling the girls, and getting started outside. If you get tired later feel free to wander over for a drink." Cari gave a wave and crossed the driveway.

Aggravated, Ray watched her go, kicking himself. "She said she wanted a clone of me, why didn't I say, 'Why settle for a clone, how about the real thing?' When am I going to step up and ask her out on a proper date?" he said to himself.

The afternoon flew by. Cari talked with the girls, filling them in on the details. They tried to reassure her that she looked great and was better off. She puttered in the yard, emptied flowerpots, turned over the vegetable garden, raked leaves, and added them to the compost pile. The sun was sinking low in the sky when Ray walked into her backyard.

Cari was happy to see him. "Are you ready for a some-thing to drink and maybe a snack? I'm starved."

"Don't go to any trouble, but I'll take a beer if you have one handy. I finished cleaning the gutters and got the firewood stacked."

"Have a seat. I'll be right back." Cari stepped into the house and ran her fingers through her hair in an attempt to smooth it. She grabbed a couple of beers and the plate of cheese and crackers and joined Ray on the deck.

Ray took the tray from her. "You shouldn't have gone to so much trouble."

"It's nothing really. If you hadn't stopped I would have put the cheese into eggs and scrambled them for dinner."

Taking a sip of her beer, she mustered up courage to ask, "Do you think I should set up another date or forget about dating?"

Surprised at the question, Ray asked, "Why, because of what happened today? Not all guys are like that dude."

"What if every guy on the dating site is looking for a quick hookup or something? I am not into casual. Is there something in my profile that would make a guy think I am?"

Ray paused, thinking how he should answer and biting back what he wanted to say. "Cari, not every guy is a jerk. Some are, but you should try again. Go out with a couple more guys and see for yourself. Don't let one jerk turn you off from all guys."

Cari had a flash of disappointment. Why didn't he ask her out?

"Well, there are one or two more guys who have contacted me who have similar interests. I guess it wouldn't hurt to send an e-mail to see if they still want to meet me. Thanks for being a good friend and encouraging me. It would be nice to have someone special in my life, and I don't have anything to lose."

Cari leaned back in the chair and closed her eyes, soaking up what was left of the afternoon sun and listening to the birds singing. Early evening shadows creeped across the deck, cooling it off quickly. They chatted about nothing in particular while they finished their drinks.

Ray sat his empty bottle on the tray. "This was nice. Maybe we can do it again soon?"

"Anytime. Have a good night." Cari stood up, awkward in the moment and not sure what to do next. She had an overwhelming urge to hug him. If Ray noticed anything, he didn't let on.

He smiled and jogged down the steps. "I'll see you later," he said and whistled off key as he went.

"Back to man shopping," she said to the night. She stood up and went inside the house to turn on her laptop.

Powering up the computer she logged onto the site. When she opened the inbox, she saw three new messages. She opened the most recent one, from Leo: he wanted to meet for coffee tomorrow. Cari quickly composed a short e-mail:

Hi Leo,

If you'd like to meet tomorrow we can grab a cup of coffee or a light lunch at the food court at the Everett Mall. I could meet you at noon. Please let me know.

Thanks,

Cari

She hit Send and went to the next message.

It was from Eddie. They had exchanged a few e-mails over the last couple of days. The subject line was "Tonight." She opened the message and read,

"Hey C-,

Wanna hook up? We can keep each other warm. If you're interested, call my cell.

Eddie

Unbelievable, she thought. She hit Reply.

NO, please don't e-mail me again. Cari.

The last e-mail was from Al.

Hey Cari,

Sorry about today. If you want to try again let me know.

Al

She hesitated for a minute.

Hi Al,

Would you like meet next Saturday? Same time and place? Just drop me an e-mail.

Cari

She was going to shut down her computer when she got an e-mail back from Leo.

Cari,

Tomorrow works, see you then.

Leo

"Tomorrow it is," Cari spoke out loud. She closed the laptop and went upstairs to choose an outfit. This was only her second date and she wasn't having fun. Instead it felt more like a job interview. Well, maybe tomorrow would be better.

Cari was waiting in the food court, and once again, she was early. She spotted Leo as he ran down the escalator. She glanced at her watch and was relieved to see that at least he was on time.

He was scanning the area for her. There weren't many people so she was easy to spot. Waving, he headed in her direction. She stood up to shake his hand but instead, he pulled her in and planted a sloppy kiss on her lips. "Excuse me!" Cari sputtered and pushed him away from her. Shaken, she wondered, who was this person and why did he think kissing her was appropriate?

Leo was oblivious to anything amiss. "Hi, it is so good to finally meet you in person." Leo grasped her outstretched hand and pumped it up and down. "I think we have a lot in common and I'm looking forward to getting to know you." Leo was dressed casually in a button-down, khakis, and loafers. "Ready for lunch?"

Furious, Cari said, "I'm sorry, Leo, I can't stay for a long lunch. Do you mind if we grab a fast food burger?" She had quickly summed him up and didn't want to be trapped any longer than was polite. He was just like Eddie, the guy looking for a quick hookup, but at least he bothered to ask her for lunch.

Clearly disappointed, he said, "Yeah, I guess so. I was hoping for something a little more than a burger." Without a look back he headed for the counter, expecting her to follow. Leo ordered and paid for his food, went back to the table and sat down.

Outraged, she turned on her heel without ordering and strode back to the table. "Leo, I seem to have lost my appetite. I'm going home. It was nice to meet you." He didn't respond or shake her extended hand. Withdrawing it, she made a beeline for the exit.

Leo yelled after her, "What, no kiss good-bye?"

Cari didn't acknowledge that she had heard him as she walked away. She got in her car and drove straight home. Thankfully, she told the girls she was going shopping and never mentioned a lunch date. She wanted to forget this one ever happened.

The week flew by and Saturday arrived. She was determined to have one cup of coffee with Al before she left the diner. When she pulled open the door she was pleased to see he was waiting for her. He stood up as she approached the table and pulled the chair out for her.

"Hi, Cari. Thank you for agreeing to meet me," Al said. "I'm sorry if I came off like a jerk last week. Friday night was a little rough and I guess I had a little too much to drink. I went out with my boys, and, well, you know how boys can be."

Cari wasn't sure how to respond to his apology. The waitress came over and took their order for coffees and muffins. Silence hung heavy in the air as the coffee cooled in the mugs. Cari attempted to fill the awkward moment with small talk about the weather.

Al cleared his throat. "Cari, I have to say, I thought you would be younger. In the pictures online you looked superhot."

Cari snapped, she had had enough of this insanity. "Well, to be honest, Al, your bio said you were much taller, and you're not. Is there anything else in your bio that isn't the truth?" Cari waited as he fumbled over his words.

Red-faced and unmistakably annoyed, he said, "Well, Cari, truth be told I don't think we're a good match. What do you say we finish our coffee and chock this up to an unsuccessful date?"

"Fine with me, I'm done now." Scraping the metal chair across the floor, she pulled a ten-dollar bill out of her wallet and threw it on the table.

"Have a nice life, Al. I hope you find what you're looking for in a woman. Oh, and Al, I never lied on my bio. You knew exactly how old I was. Good luck."

Cari stormed to her car and fumed most of the way home. Internet dating was demoralizing. She made the decision to deactivate her account. If it were meant to be someday, she would meet a nice guy. For now, she would fill her time with family, good friends, and work. She'd rather be alone than meet any more losers.

Cari pulled on to her street and saw Ray with his arms full of grocery bags. On impulse, she pulled in his driveway and slid her window down.

"Ray, if you don't have plans, would you like to come over for drinks and dinner later?"

"Yes." Surprised by the invitation, Ray quickly agreed. "Sounds great, can I bring something?"

"Just yourself and your appetite. See you at five?" Giving a wave, she backed out of the driveway.

Chapter Eleven

RAY WAS RELAXING WITH THE NEWSPAPER WHEN HIS CELL PHONE RANG. Pulling it from his pocket, he answered, "Hi, son. I didn't expect to hear from you today. I thought you guys were going to the ocean for the weekend."

"Hey, Dad, we decided to hang home. Unfortunately, I have a problem and need your help. Vanessa is camped out in front of our house and won't leave. She knocked on the door until I answered. I told her I wasn't interested in anything she had to say but she's waiting to ambush us. Any chance you could come over and get her to leave?"

"Sit tight, I'm on my way." Ray grabbed his car keys and rushed to his truck. He didn't want Jake and Sara to have to wait any longer than necessary for the cavalry to arrive. During the short drive, he remembered the conversation he had with Cari about Vanessa. Vanessa would pull out all the stops to get whatever she wanted. At the moment, it seemed like repairing her relationship with Jake was her top priority, but that was a smoke screen. He'd better get to the bottom of this situation, and fast.

Ray rounded the street corner. Vanessa's BMW was sitting at the curb, not directly in front of Jake's but close enough to have an unobstructed view of the driveway and front door. Her intent was obvious: wait until they try to leave, then pounce.

Ray parked his truck behind her and approached the car. The windows were rolled up so Vanessa didn't hear him approach. He rapped sharply on the glass and she jumped in shock. A flash of annoyance crossed her face and she turned the key to slide the window down.

"I should have known that Jake would call his daddy for help." Her voice dripped with venom and her eyes flashed with an emotion Ray couldn't read.

"What are you doing here? You do realize there are laws against stalking, right?" Ray demanded.

"Jake would never call the police on me, and I'll bet that pretty little wife of his would not understand if he tried. Sara is a sweet girl, don't you think? I met her yesterday at the convenience store." Vanessa prattled on without letting Ray get a word into the conversation. "I wouldn't have thought Mike would still be in business after all these years. I was out driving around and just happened to stop for gas, and there was Sara, we had a nice chat. She was on her way home from work and was looking forward to seeing her dear husband. Imagine my surprise when I discovered she was my daughter-in-law. It really is such a small world." Vanessa's voice dripped with faux innocence.

Ray knew by the way Vanessa wove her story she had been patiently waiting, hedging her bets that one of them would stop at Mike's on their way home. It didn't take a detective to find out where the kids lived. Any information could be found on the Internet with a few short keystrokes. Vanessa was a cat toying with a mouse and it was a game of patience—she would get the information she wanted.

"Oh, and Ray, I don't think it's against the law to sit in your car on a public street, not even in a backwoods town like Loudon."

Ray wanted to strangle her. It was on the tip of his tongue to tell her what he thought of her story when Vanessa shot Ray a victorious smile.

"I told you he'd want to see me. I am his mother after all." She nodded to the couple, walking hand in hand toward the car.

"Okay, Mother. You have us all here. Now what do you want? Tell us or leave." Jake stood next to his dad, drawing on his strength. Vanessa had always made him feel insignificant. Heaven knows Jake needed his dad when Vanessa left.

"Can't a woman want to see her only son and his beautiful young wife?" Vanessa batted her cold icy blue eyes. Her words laced with false sincerity.

"Vanessa, I've never had a mother. We aren't your family, we just happened to share the same name for a few years. We're just a page in a very old, long forgotten book. You left us in search of a rich husband and a life where you weren't responsible for a kid. What happened, did your husband finally figure out what you really are, a gold-digging witch?"

"Jake, you should reconsider how you talk to me in front of Sara. I don't want her to get the wrong impression of our relationship," Vanessa pleaded with Jake. She needed his help to get Ray on her side. What she really was desperate for was a place to hide. Using her credit cards was no longer an option.

Anger and hurt erupted from Jake. "Our relationship? Don't worry, Vanessa, Sara knows all about the kind of relationship we have. You didn't bother to show up for our wedding or even send a card. Did you have any interest to meet the woman I chose to be my wife? I guess it didn't fit into your world—telling people you had a son who was old enough to be married. Do you think I forgot when you asked me to call you 'Vanessa' instead of 'Mom' so that people wouldn't know you had a teenage son? Don't talk to me about our relationship. As far as I'm concerned, your name is on my birth certificate but you're nothing more to me than a surrogate who happens to share some DNA. End of story." Jake grabbed Sara's hand, turned on his heel, and strode back into his house, slamming their door with finality.

Vanessa saw the smile break out on Ray's face. "Well, I hope you're happy. You've turned my only child against me."

"No, Vanessa, you did that yourself, and I'm proud of the man he has become." Ray wasn't going to let her get under his skin, not this time. "Be honest with me for a change and tell me why you're really here. Maybe I can help. But you had better tell me the truth."

Vanessa heard the warning in his voice. "Ray, I am telling you the truth. I miss you and Jake. I want our family whole again. I've missed you both very much. I don't know why you find that so hard to believe." Vanessa started the car and slid the window up, quickly pulling away from the curb. As she did, she turned and looked at Ray with large crocodile tears sliding down her face. She hoped that still worked on him as it had so many times before. When Ray was a speck in her rearview mirror, she wiped away the tears and started plotting her next move. It was just a matter of time until she got what she needed from Ray and Jake.

Dumbfounded, Ray stood on the curb and watched Vanessa take off, kicking up stones in her wake. He wondered, could she really have changed, could she want a relationship with her son after all these years? No, this was Vanessa, the same person who walked out on him and Jake. It was doubtful that she wanted to be a part of their lives. "Vanessa, you might be back but I'll be watching every move you make. You won't hurt my son ever again." Ray stood ramrod straight until she disappeared.

Standing in the front window, Jake watched as his dad walked to the front door, the weight of the world resting squarely on his shoulders. Jake felt guilty he called his dad when he couldn't think of another way to get rid of his mother. Jake felt like the black cloud of his mother was hovering over them and in his gut he knew that, even if she went away, she would be back and they'd better be prepared.

When Jake looked back on his childhood he remembered Vanessa wasn't nice to anyone and could twist anything to suit her purposes. He remembered the few times he had visited her in California. Vanessa made it clear she hated everyone who worked for her new husband, Stan. Vanessa had spent countless hours trying to convince him they were stealing from them both and encouraged her husband to fire the lot of them. But Stan remained loyal, saying many of the people had worked with him for years, long before they were married. Jake recognized Vanessa wanted control over everything and everyone that came in contact with her husband, and now she was trying to do the same thing with them.

Flinging open the door, Sara rushed forward to pull her father-in-law close. "Dad, thank you so much for coming. I wasn't sure how we would get her to leave. I had just told Jake Vanessa approached me yesterday when I was pumping gas. At that time, I had no idea who she was, and she never told me. I didn't give her another thought until she got here and rang our bell." Sara was visibly shaken.

Keeping his arm around his daughter-in-law, he did his best to reassure her. "Sara there is nothing to worry about. She can't hurt us. Vanessa has always been melodramatic and wants everyone marching to her tune. She found out it's not going to work this time. She may be mad, but she'll get over it. If she comes back, call the police. If necessary we'll get a restraining order, but I don't think it will come to that. Vanessa's smart and won't want to draw that kind of attention to herself."

Ray kissed Sara's forehead and pulled both kids into a bear hug. "If you need anything, I'm a phone call away. I need to get a couple things done but I will check in with you both later." Ray crossed the lawn determined to track Vanessa down before she did anything more to upset Jake or Sara.

For the next several hours, Ray drove around the roads of Loudon and even ventured into Everett to see if he could locate her car. He needed to gain her confidence, knowing it was a line of bull about putting their family back together.

Leopards don't change their spots and Vanessa was definitely on the prowl. Ray glanced at his watch. Frustrated, he turned toward home and hoped by some miracle that Cari wasn't mad at him for being late.

When he pulled into the driveway he discovered why he didn't find Vanessa: she was parked in his driveway. He parked the truck as she got out of her car. He could see she had been crying, her eyes were rimmed in red and mascara had left black streaks down her face.

"Vanessa, how long have you been here? I've been looking everywhere for you. Talk to me tell me what's really going on. Maybe I can help. We used to be friends and we could talk about anything." Ray chose his words carefully as he stopped six feet in front of her. He didn't want her to get the wrong impression about what he was offering.

Vanessa was clutching her large designer bag with her right hand tucked out of view. Ray glanced at the bag. Slowly, she withdrew a small handgun.

Vanessa wiped her tears away with the back of her hand. "Ray, why do you always have to be so difficult? All I wanted to do was roll back time and have you and Jake in my life again. I've made mistakes but I want to make it up to you both. You're all I have."

In a split second Ray was horrified to realize this wasn't the same woman who walked out on him, something had happened over the years and she had become unbalanced. His cell phone vibrated in his pocket and he itched to answer it.

"Vanessa, it's my cell phone and I'd like to check and see who it is. If it's Jake, he'll wonder what's going on if I don't answer and come over. I think we should spend some time by ourselves for now, talking, don't you agree?"

Vanessa thought about it and nodded in agreement. The display read "CARI." Faking enthusiasm, he answered, "Hey, Jake, guess what? I found your mom. Yup, that's right, she's standing right in front of me. We're going to have a nice long conversation and see if we can figure out a way to get beyond the past and be a family again."

Ray heard the confusion in her voice when Cari said, "Ah, Ray . . . it's me. Cari."

"Jake, I know you're a little skeptical but give your mom and me a chance to talk. Yup, she's here with me right now. She standing right in front of me." Ray was smiling, praying Cari would figure out something was terribly wrong.

"Ray, are you okay?" she quizzed.

"No, I'm a little tired. But I have to go for now." Ray paused, hoping she had read between the lines and would send help. The situation with Vanessa had quickly gone from bad to worse. "That's right, son. Your mom and I are going to talk. Let's plan on getting together tomorrow night. I think we're going to be pretty involved for the next few hours. I'll talk to you later, Jake."

Pausing again, as if Jake was asking him a question, "Yes, I'll call you later, after mom and I have had a chance to talk." Ray didn't wait for Cari to respond. He hit the Disconnect button and slipped the phone into his shirt pocket.

Cari stared at the phone. What was going on over there? It didn't take a genius to figure out something was terribly wrong. She immediately dialed 911 and gave the dispatcher a brief overview of her conversation, asking for the police to come without sirens or lights. She hung up and headed out the back door, looking for something to carry, like a weapon, but all she could find was a steel rake. Grabbing it, she took off at a dead run. Cari wasn't about to waste precious minutes waiting for the police. Cari skirted around the edge of the yard and up the back side of the house, doing her best to stay hidden. She peeked around the corner and her blood ran cold. Vanessa was standing in the middle of the driveway, holding a gun pointed directly at the center of Ray's chest. For a second fear paralyzed her but then adrenaline kicked in. She had to create a distraction before Vanessa pulled the trigger.

Chapter Twelve

"HELLOOOOO," CARI YELLED AS SHE CROSSED THE GRASS, trying to look casual while making a bee-line for Ray and Vanessa. Her heart was hammering in her throat. She didn't know what else to do but try and distract Vanessa, giving the police time to arrive. Could she get Vanessa to drop the gun? Was that even a possibility? Cari saw Vanessa looked half-crazed. What if she couldn't think of a way to save Ray?

Ray heard Cari yelling as she trotted through the yard. He cringed; he desperately wanted to holler for her to run. How was he going to protect her from this madness? In a matter of minutes, Vanessa's gun would be trained on both of them.

Ray looked at Vanessa and whispered, "Don't worry, I'll get rid of her and we can finish our conversation."

Barely containing her rage, Vanessa spoke in a low voice, "You'd better or her blood is on your hands."

Cari sauntered up with a rake slung over her shoulder, looking like she didn't have a care in the world. Doing her best not to let on that she saw the gun she kept her tone light. Cari flashed a bright smile at Vanessa and turned her attention to Ray. "Hello, you guys. Ray, I finished with your rake, thanks for letting me borrow it. I was going to put it in my shed when I remembered you said you were doing yard work today. I can't imagine what happened to mine." Cari rambled on as she carefully scoped out the situation. "I hope I'm not interrupting anything."

Cari locked eyes with Ray, wishing she could tell him help was on the way.

Deliberately turning her back on Ray, Cari put herself in front of the gun. "Vanessa, it's nice to see you again. I wasn't sure if you were still in town. I'm sure your husband is anxious for you to get back home."

Vanessa casually tucked her right hand inside the bag. Cari glanced in that direction, trying to determine where the gun was pointed.

"Cari, forgive me if I don't feel the same way. It isn't nice to see you again. Now if you want to put the rake down and leave us, we have things to discuss that don't concern you." Her left hand let go of the shoulder strap as she gestured to the garage door. "You can put the rake over there. I don't think Ray will be doing yard work today."

Cari had to stall for more time. She prayed a police car was driving up the street, coming to their rescue. If more leaves were off the trees, the sounds from North Main Street would be drifting their way.

Ignoring Vanessa, Cari babbled on. "Wasn't it a beautiful day today! It was a great day to work outside. It was sunny and the air was so fresh, crisp, and clean. I just love fall. Vanessa you must miss the fall weather when you're out west. I'm sure the weather is always perfect. At least that's what I've always heard. What do you think?"

Visibly agitated, Vanessa was quickly losing control of the tenuous hold she had on her anger. "Cari, I don't care if you think I'm rude but put the rake down and leave. Ray and I are in the middle of an important conversation. And for the record, the west coast isn't all it's cracked up to be," she said with disgust.

Cari glanced at Ray, mentally preparing both of them. This might be their only chance to get the gun away from Vanessa.

Ray was scared, not for himself but for Cari. He didn't want her taking any risks because of him. Horrified, he watched as if in slow motion as Cari grabbed the rake at the top of the handle with her left hand and in one hard, fast motion let it land squarely across the bag Vanessa was holding, attempting to knock the gun away and force Vanessa to the ground. Ray sprang forward, landing on Vanessa in a desperate attempt to wrestle the gun away. A muffled pop could be heard as the three struggled. A police car screamed into the driveway, coming to a halt and spraying gravel everywhere.

An officer rushed over and pulled Ray, Cari, and Vanessa up from the ground, fearing that Ray had the gun. Blood was everywhere. In those first few moments it was unclear who had been shot. Vanessa was freaking out, screaming that her husband tried to kill her. Cari struggled to get the officer's attention. He had to know Vanessa had the gun, not the other way around.

Holding his belly, Ray croaked "Cari" as he slid to the ground.

"Call an ambulance!" Cari rushed to Ray, who was lying on the ground, blood seeping, unchecked, from between his fingers. She didn't know what to do but place her hands over his, applying pressure to the wound. Another cruiser pulled in and an officer hurried to Cari's side, providing assistance until the EMTs could get to the scene. Vanessa was crying hysterically. She had been placed in handcuffs and was sitting in the back of the cruiser and shouting her innocence and that Cari had the gun and had shot Ray.

Cari moved to hold Ray's head between her hands, softly talking to him and begging him to hang on. An officer held a bandage on his belly wound, keeping the pressure on it to staunch the torrent of blood. Cari's heart filled with anguish. She couldn't waste time crying, there would be time for that later. At this moment, Ray needed her to be calm and clear-headed.

"Where is the ambulance?" she demanded.

"The bus is two minutes out, Cari. Hang in there, Ray."

For the first time, it registered that her old friend Hank Bosse, one of Loudon's finest, was next to her. Hank was a regular at the shop for coffee and conversation. He was also a good friend of Ray's so it hadn't taken him long to size up the situation. Flashing red lights bounced off the garage as the ambulance halted. Two EMTs jumped out. Sue Jones from the passenger side went directly over to Ray while her partner, Tim Wells, pulled gear and the gurney from the back.

"Cari, can you tell me what happened?" Sue was checking Ray's pulse, listening to his heart and lungs. She lifted the bandage and quickly cut away his shirt, assessing how much damage the gunshot had inflicted.

Keeping her professionalism, Sue replaced the makeshift bandage with a new one. She instructed Cari to hold her hand on it firmly as they lifted Ray to the gurney. "It is critical we get him to the hospital quickly. He needs surgery."

Tim collapsed the gurney. Hank slipped his hands under Ray's head and helped lift him from the cold ground, moving to the open doors of the ambulance to gently place him on a gurney. They firmly locked it. Sue climbed in the back just seconds before Hank slammed the doors shut. Tim leaped into the driver's seat and rolled out of the driveway, heading to the hospital in Everett.

Hank turned to study Cari; she was standing still as a statue. He gently touched her arm. "Cari, are you hurt?" He could see she was in shock. "I'm sorry, Cari, but I have to ask you a few questions. We need to transport Mrs. Fisher to the station and I'd like to have a few more facts before we book her."

Cari mentally pulled herself together. "I'm okay, Hank, but I need to get to the hospital. Can we do this later? Will you call Jake?"

"Cari, I know you want to get to the hospital but I need to get your statement now so that I can book Ray's ex-wife." Hank was firm as he spoke.

"Alright, I want to make sure Vanessa won't be going anywhere but to jail." Cari's knees grew shaky. "I'm sorry. Is it okay if I sit down for a few minutes?"

Hank and another officer, Pete Kaplan, each took an arm and escorted her to the front steps. Cari dropped her head between her knees and took gulps of air, willing the light-headed feeling to leave her.

Questions and answers flowed between the police and Cari. Hank was alarmed when Cari told him Vanessa had tried to break into Ray's house. "I guess she didn't leave town like Ray had hoped." Taking a deep breath, Cari stood up and swayed slightly. Hank reached out to steady her. "Can I go now? I really need to get to the hospital, just in case Ray needs something."

"Yes, however, you'll need to come down to the station and give a sworn statement, but that doesn't need to be done today. I can assure you Vanessa will spend the night in jail and she'll be charged. Assault with a deadly weapon and anything else that we think might apply."

"Captain, I'll head over to Jake's and make sure that he and Sara get to the hospital safely."

Hank nodded in agreement. "Can I drive you to the hospital, call the girls or Shane?"

She gave him a sad smile. "Thanks, Hank. I'll be fine. I'll call my kids. If I don't feel up to driving, one of them will come get me. If you need me for anything else I'll be at the hospital."

Before Hank could say another word Cari was on her way to her house in the quickly falling darkness, dinner forgotten. She didn't notice her blood-covered clothes. She moved on autopilot. She had to make sure Ray would be okay.

She pulled her keys off the hook, shocked to see her hands were covered in dried blood. Dashing to the sink, she dumped dish soap over her hands, vigorously scrubbing them under steaming hot water. Satisfied, she grabbed her bag, jumped into the car, and tore out of the driveway. Her cell phone was buried deep in her bag and it could stay there until she reached the hospital. She'd have plenty of time when she got to the emergency room for phone calls.

Fearing the worst, she parked the car and hesitantly walked through the sliding doors. She could picture Ray being wheeled through these doors just a short time ago. Jake and Sara were sitting in the waiting area, holding each other's hands and talking with Hank. The moment Jake saw Cari he rose and went to her, his arms pulling her close to him.

Choked with emotion, he said, "I've been told you saved my father's life. I will never be able to thank you enough."

A doctor entered the waiting room. "Mr. Davis? I'm Dr. Newhouse, the emergency room physician." He shook Jake's hand. "I have examined your father and he's lost a lot of blood, but the good news is the bullet passed through and missed all his vital organs. It was also a very small caliber so the internal damage was minimal. We're giving him a transfusion, and we'll have to perform surgery to repair the damage but your father is very strong and in excellent health. I don't expect any complications. We're prepping him now and will be taking him down to surgery shortly. You can see him for a few minutes. He's been given pain meds so he's awake but a bit groggy. Remember, he is very weak, please limit this visit to a couple of minutes."

He turned to Cari asking, "Are you Mrs. McKenna?"

Cari nodded slowly.

"Mr. Davis has been asking for you. He's very agitated and needs to be reassured you're safe. If his son agrees, you can go in for a moment when he's done."

The doctor moved through the automatic doors to check on his patient. Jake grasped Cari's hand. "Go first. It will help once he sees you standing in front of him."

Riddled with guilt, Cari cried, "Jake, this is my fault. If

it hadn't been for me foolishly thinking I could take the gun away from Vanessa he wouldn't have gotten shot. I don't know what I was thinking, how could I disarm a lunatic?"

"Cari, if you hadn't tried there is no telling what Vanessa would have done. Hank said you risked your life, that you put yourself between the gun and Dad. We could never blame you." Jake did his best to console her.

Sara stood next to her husband. Gently, she pushed Cari to the door. "Go. Let Ray see for himself that you're fine. It will help him and you'll feel better, too."

Cari rubbed sweaty palms on her jeans and nervously ran her fingers through her hair. She pushed through the heavy door and found Ray in a large cubicle lying on a stark white bed, surrounded by machines beeping and recording every bodily function. She got a little woozy when she saw the transfusion line dripping life into his arm. She put a hand on the wall to steady herself before going to his bedside.

"Hey, neighbor, can I get you a cup of coffee with your IV?" Cari took his cool hand in hers and he lightly squeezed it.

He struggled to open his eyes and tried to focus on her. Tears slipped from the corners, sliding to the stiff white pillowcase. His face blended too well with the bedsheets. Ray moved his lips and Cari leaned in to his in an attempt to hear what he was saying.

Ray's voice, a hoarse whisper, croaked, "Are you hurt? You have blood on your shirt."

She held tight to his hand. "No, you got the worst of it, not me." She gave him a tender smile and kept listening.

"You saved me. How did you know she had a gun?" Due to the pain medication his words came out slowly.

"I saw the outline of the barrel against her bag and I just needed to hit her hard enough so I'd knock her over. Who would have thought you'd jump her, trying to be the hero?" Cari teased softly.

Giving her a weak smile, he said, "It's the man's job to protect the womenfolk."

"We can talk about those old-fashioned ideas of yours later. For now, rest and when you're in a room I'll come see you. Jake and Sara are outside waiting to see you."

She leaned over and placed a tender kiss on his forehead. He tugged on her fingers as she pulled her hand away and slipped out of the room.

"Jake, he's waiting for you."

Oblivious to everything around her, Cari collapsed in a worn plastic chair, dropped her head in her hands, and sobbed. Four sets of arms slid around her and held her while she cried.

While she was with Ray, her kids had arrived. Jake and Sara had given them an abbreviated version of what happened, making sure they knew Cari saved Ray's life.

The gravity of what had occurred struck the core of the McKenna family. If things had been different, it would be their mother getting ready for surgery. The kids were proud of her. Cari needed her children to get through the next several hours.

For now, all they could do was hold her tight and let her cry until the tears were done.

The two families moved to the waiting area outside the surgical suite. Time dragged on for an eternity.

Breaking the silence, Ellie said to the group, "We're going to go find the vending machines. Does anyone want a shot of caffeine?" She needed to keep busy, the waiting was driving her crazy.

Everyone agreed they could use a drink. "Kate, do you want to come with me?" Kate got up and accompanied her sister to the cafeteria. After they all had donated blood, all that was left for the family to do was wait. Shane was sitting with Cari, his arm draped loosely around her shoulders. Sara and Jake were across the aisle, leaned back in chairs, holding hands with their eyes closed.

Shane avoided looking at his mother's shirt. It was a sharp reminder of how dangerous the situation had been.

Kate and Ellie, in search of cookies and coffee, were finally free to talk about the events of the day.

"What do you think got into Mom? Do you think she intended to take out a crazy person?" Ellie demanded. "She could have died."

"Ellie, think about it. Mom had one person on her mind: Ray. Her instincts kicked in and she reacted the only way she could. She wasn't going to stand around twiddling her thumbs waiting for the police. Whether she admits it or not, she is in love with Ray and has been for a long time. Right now she doesn't understand why she put herself in harm's way, but at some point she'll figure it out."

"How can she not know how she feels? I thought when a person's in love they feel it, understand it, and want it."

"When Daddy died she was left with a huge void in her life. Over the years her relationship with Ray has slowly developed. You know that Mom talks to Dad. They were best friends and lovers. That's rare to find it once in a life-time, let alone twice. There were times I believed you only found it if you were really lucky. Ray walking into Mom's life is the exception. When they are both ready, they'll figure it out, but I think fate just kicked them both in the butt." Kate smiled at Ellie and tweaked her nose. "We should get back. Everyone will be wondering where we ran off to."

Ellie shook her head. "I still think Mom would know if she were in love. But since I've never been in love how can I know for certain?"

The girls walked into the waiting room. Jake and Sara were talking to the surgeon, Dr. Peters. Jake motioned for everyone to join them.

Dr. Peters spoke to the facts regarding Ray's condition. "He came through the surgery with no complications. As we thought, the bullet did minimal damage and we were able to repair the damage. We will give him another pint of blood and he'll be on heavy painkillers for the next twelve hours to keep him comfortable, so expect him to sleep. We're going to keep him in intensive care overnight as a precaution. If all goes well, he will be up and around tomorrow and should be able to go home in a few days." Dr. Peters paused momentarily, waiting for questions.

"Doctor, when will he get moved to the ICU?" Cari inquired.

"Roughly thirty minutes. Once he gets settled he can have one visitor at a time for ten minutes each hour, and immediate family only."

Looking to make his point, Dr. Peters looked around the group, not sure who was immediate family. "If you have any questions, the duty nurse knows how to find me. I'll be back to check on him a bit later."

Jake extended his hand. "Thank you, Dr. Peters. We all appreciate what you did for my dad."

Shane extended his hand and said, "Thank you, Doctor."

A loud sob of relief escaped Cari. Shane and Jake hurried to her side and helped her to a vacant chair.

Concerned, Shane asked, "Mom, do you need something?"

Shane and Jake vigorously rubbed her cold, clammy hands. Her emotions came crashing down. Feeling overwhelmed, Cari didn't have the strength to sort through any feelings at the moment.

"I think the shock is kicking in. I just need to sit down for a minute. Stop worrying, please." She gave a tentative smile to the boys.

"We should be going. Jake, you and Sara need to go upstairs and we'll check in tomorrow," Shane said. He wanted to get his mother home before she collapsed from exhaustion.

Feeling steadier, Cari stood up. "I agree. Jake, your dad is going to want to see you both, so go ahead. I'll call you tomorrow. "

"What? Cari, you can't leave! Dad will have my hide if you're not here when he wakes up. He specifically told me he needed to see you again after the surgery, even if I had to tie you to a chair." Jake was adamant, "We stay together. The McKennas are the closest thing I've ever had to family except for Sara. Please stay with us," he implored. "I don't know what we would have done without you the last few hours."

Cari laid her cool hands on Jake's and Sara's cheeks. "We'll stay, as long as you need us."

The next thirty minutes dragged. Shane went to the nurse's station in an attempt to get information about when Ray would be able to have visitors. Cari couldn't hear the conversation but relief washed over her when he returned and gave a thumbs-up.

Shane sat down next to his mother. "It won't be much longer. They need to get him settled."

Restless, Jake stood up and started to pace. He saw Ray being wheeled down the hall with bottles hanging above him. Jake moved to the observation window, which gave him a full view of the patients. The nurses moved Ray into the hospital bed. His dad was deathly pale and not moving. It was comforting to see the heart monitor beeping on the wall, strong and steady. He wondered what his mother had been thinking, carrying a gun? At some point, he would go to the police station and try to figure out what had happened. The most important thing moving forward was to get Vanessa out of their lives permanently.

Jake kept a watchful eye on the nurse who was hovering over Ray, adjusting the tubes attached to his arm and the wires that disappeared under the gown he wore. She looked up, sent him a reassuring smile, and held up a finger indicating she would be done momentarily.

"Mr. Davis, you can come in. I'm Josie, a registered nurse specializing in trauma patients. I'll be taking care of your dad until seven tomorrow morning." The nurse escorted Jake into the ICU. "I want to reassure you to not be alarmed at his condition. The machines make a lot of noise but everything is connected to my workstation where I can monitor your dad's vitals. He's stable and will be awake soon but the anesthesia and pain meds will keep him groggy for a few more hours."

She paused, alert to Jake's reaction. She continued, "I know it can be a shock when you see someone in the ICU the first time. You can come in and sit with him as often as you like since he is the only patient. However, if we get additional patients we will need to restrict you to ten minutes every hour. But we'll cross that bridge if we need to. Remember, he's in here for tonight as a precaution. He lost a lot of blood and we want to keep a close eye on him."

"Thank you. I appreciate the time you took to explain everything, Josie. I'm going to sit with him and ask Cari to come in. She saved his life today and I think he didn't believe us when we told him she wasn't hurt. The last time he saw her, well, she was covered in blood."

The nurse left the semidarkened room, illuminated only with the light over Ray's bed. Jake sat in a chair next to the bed, his fingers clenched. Patience had never been one of his best traits and he hadn't developed any today. Exhausted his eyes closed in an attempt to stop the burning sensation. It felt like a lifetime ago that his mother sat outside his house and his father came to help. He thought about Cari. If anyone was to blame, it was him. He should have dealt with his mother like an adult.

Ray stirred in the bed and groaned softly.

Jake flew out of the chair. "Dad, relax, I'm here." He placed a comforting hand on Ray's arm in an attempt to penetrate the anesthesia haze.

Confused, Ray struggled to open his eyes. "Son? Did a truck run over me? And my head it hurts like hell."

In a soothing voice, Jake reassured him, "Dad, easy. You're in the hospital. Do you remember Vanessa shooting you?"

Everything came rushing back. Ray tried to sit up,

groaning in pain as he fell back on the bed. "Where's Cari? Is she alright? I need to save her." Jake was surprised, he knew that his father liked and respected Cari but now he suspected it was something more than friendship.

"Dad, Cari's fine. She saved your life by hitting Vanessa with the rake. Don't you remember?"

Ray smiled, he vaguely remembered Cari whipping the rake off her shoulder and smacking Vanessa with it. What a spitfire, he thought as he drifted off to sleep.

CB CB CB CB CB CB CB CB

When Ray woke, Cari was sitting beside him, lightly caressing his hand. "Hey, sleepy head. Did you have a nice nap?"

Ray focused on a pair of beautiful green eyes. He mumbled "hi" before succumbing to heavy lids and drifted off again, but hunger penetrated the deep sleep. Ray woke to find Cari asleep in a chair next to his bed. It was comforting to hear her slow, deep breathing. Relieved, he turned toward the window, happy to see a new day.

"Cari?" Ray whispered.

Cari sprang into action. "What? Are you okay, are you in pain, do you want a sip of water, should I call the nurse?" The questions tumbled out of her in quick succession. Concern clouded her eyes.

"I'm fine, a little sore and maybe a little hungry. Do you think I could get something to eat? We didn't get to have our dinner," he teased.

Cari was relieved. It was the best thing she had heard in the last eighteen hours.

"I'm sure the nurse can rustle something up," she said and went to check.

Cari returned with a bounce in her step. "Good news. Broth and Jell-O coming right up."

"That's it? I've been shot and all I get is broth? I deserve a four-course meal or something, don't ya think?" Gingerly, he shrugged his shoulders and continued, "I guess it's a start. Will you stay for a while?"

"Since you asked so nicely, I can hang around. After all, somebody has to look after you," she teased.

Ray settled back into his pillows to wait for breakfast and enjoy the view.

Chapter Thirteen

RAY QUICKLY REGAINED HIS STRENGTH TO THE POINT where he was anxious to get out of the hospital and desperate to get back into a routine. The doctors informed him it would be several weeks before he could go back to work. Sitting around watching daytime television was going to drive him nuts and he was worried about Cari's house needing to be finished before the first snow.

When the day arrived that he was to be discharged, he waited impatiently for Jake to pick him up. He needed to see Cari. He didn't need to be reminded that when Vanessa held him at gunpoint, Cari rushed to his side, saving him in spite of the risk. Over the last couple of days Ray and Cari had talked about that day and Cari had been blunt, pointing out that he hadn't been in control of the situation and there had been no way of knowing if or when Vanessa would pull the trigger. Cari informed Ray she did exactly what needed to be done and would do it again. Ray understood why she did it but it didn't make the memory less frightening.

During the last few days he had come to realize his life could be over in a heartbeat. He couldn't bear to watch Cari go out on any more first dates. His timing could be better but Vanessa showed him time waits for no man. Cari had his heart and it was time she knew it.

Jake was running behind schedule. He had stopped by the police station to talk with Hank Bosse and had been informed Vanessa was moved to the county detention facility without bail, pending her court appearance. It was obvious she wasn't mentally stable. Hank had arranged medical and psychiatric care for her.

Hank requested Ray come to the police station when he was discharged from the hospital. They needed to add Ray's statement to the official record. Wishing he could delay the inevitable, Jake had hoped to buy a little more time.

Ray sat in a plastic chair next to the open window, drinking in the fresh air and thinking about Vanessa. What do you say to someone you once loved who just tried to kill you? He couldn't wrap his head around being held at gunpoint, especially by Vanessa—she always hated guns. How could he put this behind him and move on with life? Would he ever understand what had gone so wrong that would lead her to do this despicable act? Lost in thought, he didn't see Jake standing in the doorway.

"Hey, Dad. Are you ready to bug out of here? We can stop by Cari's for coffee and a blueberry muffin." Hoping to see a smile instead of a frown, he dangled What's Perkin' as a bribe.

"I'm ready, but first we're going to the jail." Ray had made one decision: He would no longer refer to Vanessa as Jake's mother, she didn't deserve the privilege. Determined to get the interview over with, he stood up too fast, swaying as he struggled to regain his balance. "We need to get this behind us."

"Hank wants to tell you in person what he has discovered during the investigation." Jake gave his dad a hard look. "You know this isn't going to be easy to hear."

Before Ray could respond, Josie popped into the room pushing a wheelchair. Ray glared at her, "You're kidding, right?"

Suppressing a laugh, she said, "Hospital rules, pal. Hop in and you'll be out of here in a flash."

Ray looked at Jake. "Son, I beg you. Please, tell this very nice nurse I can walk to the elevator without the use of a wheelchair."

With a shrug of his shoulders, Jake smiled. "Rules, Dad. I'll push. It'll be good practice when you're like a hundred."

Ray snorted and grudgingly plunked into the chair. Jake whistled as they strolled to the elevator.

"You're enjoying this a little too much, don't you think?" Ray muttered but then relaxed. A wheelchair ride was a small price for freedom.

CB CB CB CB CB CB CB CB

At the police station, Jake pulled up a chair for his dad and went in search of bottled water. When he returned, Hank and Ray were catching up as old friends do.

"I'm looking forward to sleeping in my own bed," Ray said as he tried to keep the conversation light in spite of the reason why they were sitting in a cop house.

Hank waited for Jake to sit down. He cleared his throat. "I know I'm stating the obvious but, in a nutshell, Vanessa had a breakdown. We have been in touch with the authorities in California and learned her husband, Stan, had been very sick and one day she up and left."

Ray didn't look overly surprised. "That's what she does best."

Hank held up his hand. "Stan was admitted to the hospital, where they ran some tests and discovered he was being poisoned, very slowly. Vanessa had been giving him small doses of eyedrops over an extended period, which of course made him violently ill. They believe she was slipping them into his juice. Based on his statement, Stan wasn't getting better and asked to see the doctor. The exact sequence of events are a little hazy but it sounds like he collapsed and she took off. Lucky for Stan, his secretary was concerned when she tried calling their home and cell phones and when she didn't get an answer, she went over. When no one came to the door, she broke a window. She found him unresponsive on the bedroom floor and called for an ambulance." Hank paused, it was clear that Jake and Ray were stunned.

"The bottom line: Vanessa is wanted in California for attempted murder. After our interrogation, she broke down and said she killed Stan. That's why she came back to Loudon. For some reason she thought if she could create the illusion that you two had been trying to reconcile, she'd avoid being accused of murder. Vanessa said she only wanted to make him sick so he wouldn't ask for a divorce. From what I've discovered, things haven't been good between them for a long time and I think the strain of believing she killed him pushed her over the edge."

Silence hung heavy in the room. The only sound to be heard was the clock ticking on the wall.

Ray took a long drink of water. Suppressing a shudder that ran down his spine, he croaked, "How could she have gone so far that she'd try to kill someone? First Stan, then me, do you think she would have tried to harm Jake?" Distractedly, Ray ran his hands through his hair, hanging his head. "I guess the only comfort we have now is that she's behind bars and hopefully she can't hurt anyone again."

"Ray, there is no way to tell what her plan would have been for Jake. We can all be thankful we will never have to find out. I don't think Vanessa will be out of jail for quite some time, between the charges here and in California."

"Very sad. This whole mess is just sad." Jake shook his head in disbelief. He was glad his dad was with him when he heard the news. "How could this be my mother? Granted she's never been much of a real mother but she is mine. It's going to take a very long time for me to begin to understand why she poisoned Stan and then set Dad up for her alibi."

Ray turned to Jake. "Get the car. It's time we see her." His mouth was set in a thin straight line.

Hank stood up. "Give me a couple of minutes, and I'll make a call and arrange for you to see her."

ରେ ରେ ରେ ରେ ରେ ରେ ରେ ରେ

The door clanged shut behind Vanessa. She was curious to see Jake and Ray sitting at the visitor's table. "I'm surprised to see you both. Why are you here?" On some level, she knew Ray would come to her. Locking eyes with Ray, she saw they were like granite, cold and hard.

She shuffled to the table. The heavy chair grated against the concrete floor. Once seated, she placed handcuffed wrists on the cold metal table. "I don't think you'll understand what I've been through, but I am truly sorry for what happened and I hope you can forgive me," she said contritely. Vanessa glanced up at both of them to see if she could read their reaction. Nothing—they stared at her. The silence was oppressive.

After a time, Ray drummed his fingers on the table, hoping something would come to him that would be productive. "Vanessa, we know about Stan. What were you thinking? Giving him eyedrops to make him sick, are you insane?" Venom dripped from Ray's words.

"Don't you dare judge me!" Vanessa's anger flashed. "You have no idea what my life was like with him. Stan was always off doing things without me and I was left on my own all the time, with the exception of certain occasions when he needed a wife to go to some stupid dinner with his friends or family. It was never about me—always Stan, Stan, Stan. And I was window dressing," she said bitterly.

Vanessa spoke her husband's name with contempt.

"I have had a hard time believing that your life was so terrible it drove you to try and kill your husband. It was the life you craved, everything you dreamed about—money, position, and a life of ease."

Vanessa was silent, staring at her hands.

"Why come back here? When we divorced, did you think I would carry a torch for you the rest of my life? I made a good life for Jake and myself. We have amazing friends that are like family and we have a great life." Ray didn't need answers but he wanted her to know he was finished.

"I needed an alibi, and everyone respects and trusts you, Ray. If anyone could help me, it would have been you. I thought I could tell you Stan was trying to get rid of me and you'd help. I thought our history was the key to solving all my problems." Emotionless, Vanessa stated her version of the truth.

Ray ignored her and continued, "The only good thing that came from our marriage is sitting next to me. I'm grateful to you for Jake. You need to get help and someday maybe you'll realize how badly you screwed up your life with these controlling, manipulative actions. Good luck, Vanessa, you're going to need it."

Jake watched his mother. She was a stranger to him. "Vanessa, I have nothing to say to you except that if I could take your DNA out of my body I would. You're not my mother; you are just a lady who gave birth to me. I have one parent and he's sitting next to me." Jake deliberately pushed back his chair and stood up. "Dad, it's time to go. We're done here."

Without another word, father and son turned their backs on her and moved to the door.

"Jake! Wait, I need you to forgive me." Vanessa became unglued, begging for him to stop. She reached out and grabbed at Jake's jacket. The guard stepped between Vanessa and Jake, restraining her.

"Visitation is over. It's time to go back to your cell," the guard ordered. Vanessa continued to struggle in an attempt to reach Jake but the guard was immovable. "Fisher, let's go. Now!"

Finally, Vanessa was firmly escorted to the security door and led back to the cellblock. It shut behind her with a loud bang.

Ray and Jake could hear Vanessa screaming through the door, pleading for them to come back. Ray draped his arm around his son's shoulders and held him as he once again mourned the loss of his mother.

CR CR CR CR CR CR CR CR

Arriving home, father and son were drained. Ray noticed everything outside looked normal; there were no physical signs of the shooting. A note from Cari was propped on the counter: directions for heating up the casserole that was waiting in the refrigerator. There was a basket of fresh muffins and the coffee pot was ready to brew. He was disappointed. He had hoped she would be waiting for him.

CR CR CR CR CR CR CR CR

It seemed like weeks when in reality it was a few days before Ray saw Cari. Each time he walked past the kitchen window his eyes were drawn to her backyard. He had been feeling out of sorts, unable to pick up the phone to call her. He couldn't figure out what was stopping him, until he saw her raking leaves with the autumn sun reflecting rays of gold off her hair, and then it registered in the pit of his stomach. He was carrying around a heavy load of guilt.

Ray stepped out the back door into the cool afternoon air. "Cari!" he shouted.

Cari heard her name and glanced over. There he was, standing tall and waving enthusiastically. She didn't need see his blue eyes, she felt them capture her heart. She casually made her way to Ray, vowing to keep the conversation light. She had been avoiding him, confused about her feelings and what possessed her to jump in between a loaded gun and this man.

"Hi. How are you feeling?" Cari cautiously embraced him, being careful not to put pressure on his wounds. "You look a lot better than the last time I saw you."

Ray was overwhelmed with the scent of lilac that clung to her hair and the fresh scent of the outdoors. He had forgotten how wonderful she smelled.

"I am better. I wanted to thank you for everything. I was hoping you'd come over so we could talk. Jake and I went to see Vanessa. But most important, I wanted to tell you again how grateful I am that you used yourself as a human shield." Ray's blue eyes were filled with emotion. He didn't think it was in his best interest to break down in front of the bravest woman he knew.

"Please have a cup of coffee with me?" Ray slid open the glass door and gestured for her to go inside. She stepped over the threshold and they sat at the kitchen table. Ray fiddled with the coffee pot.

"I'm not sure where to start. I guess, illogically, from the recent past and work toward the present. It seems Vanessa was slowly poisoning Stan, her husband. In a twisted way, she was trying to avoid a divorce, but swears she didn't want to kill him. They had been having problems for over a year. Supposedly, Vanessa read the handwriting on the wall. About three weeks ago, she accidently she gave him too much of whatever it was and took off, thinking she killed him. Desperate to hide from the authorities, she headed east, thinking no one would look for her in Loudon."

Horrified, Cari said, "Oh my stars, how is Stan?"

"The good news is she only succeeded in making him violently ill, and he'll make a full recovery. His secretary found him in time, and got him to the hospital. I don't think Vanessa 'taking care of' Stan will stop the divorce proceedings now." The irony wasn't lost on Cari or Ray.

Instinctively, Cari knew Ray needed to talk. She had questions but there would be time for those later.

"Jake and I were a cover story. She didn't want to establish a relationship with Jake and Sara, and she didn't want me back. She was praying that if someone came around asking if she had been in town Jake and I would lie for her, giving her a solid alibi. Sadly, Jake told her he doesn't have a mother, that this is a single-parent family. I'm sorry he feels motherless but I completely understand and support him. When he thinks about the gun and Vanessa talking to Sara at the convenience store, his blood runs cold. I've reminded him that Sara is safe and no one is going to hurt her. I wish

I could say something to keep his mind from wandering to what might have happened. But, to be honest, I've gone down the same crazy train of thought regarding what could have happened to all of us."

Ray toyed with his empty cup. "I guess Vanessa thought the gun would scare me into helping her.

Frankly, I can't believe how messy everything got, from her coming here, to showing up at the kids house and then shooting me. Putting it mildly, things didn't go the way Vanessa planned. When she took off and I tried to find her, I wanted to convince her to stay away from Jake. The day of the shooting I wanted to ask Vanessa to be patient if she really wanted to have a relationship with Jake, that it would take some patience on her side. But she vanished, only to be waiting for me here. And we all know how well that turned out."

Ray stopped talking, got up, and wandered to the front window that overlooked the driveway. Coffee was forgotten. Staring at the spot where everything unraveled he took a deep ragged breath before he finished the story.

"Vanessa thought if she spent enough time with Jake I would help her get out of the hole she had dug. She grew more agitated when my cell rang. I've wracked my brain trying to figure out why she let me answer it. Was she hoping it was Jake? I'll never know but I'm grateful she did."

Ray turned away from the window and gave Cari a hard look. "I know we've been through this already but what possessed you to rush over? I thought you'd call the police and wait. Did you stop to think about what you might be walking into? And then you bring a rake. Did you think that was a great weapon choice?" Ray was half teasing, half serious. "You looked fearless."

Cari moved to stand next to him. "Ray, I didn't have a lot of time to formulate a plan. I grabbed what was handy and I didn't think a rake would make her suspicious. First, I snuck around the opposite side of the house so I could see what was going on. Then, the adrenaline kicked in or something and I wasn't going to leave you waiting for the police. So, I played it by ear and acted natural, coming around the house like I've done thousands of other times. Since I was acting the way I did when she was trying to break in, Vanessa didn't give it another thought. And, she was too wrapped up with what was going on in her head to pay much attention to me. Then you had to rush her, the gun went off, and there was blood everywhere. For a brief second, I prayed she shot herself. But when I realized it was you, I lost it. You were bleeding, the police were there, and then everything blurs together." Cari couldn't forget holding Ray's head in her lap and the fear that smothered her. At that moment, déjà vu slammed her and she suddenly saw the truth. She was in love with Ray Davis!

Ray was standing inches from her, watching her relive the shooting and witnessing the pain, and then something else flashed across her face, something he couldn't read.

"I have to go. The girls are coming over to look at paint swatches. We should talk about the sunroom, maybe tomorrow after work or something. The boys—Shane, Don, and Jake—have been working at the house every night since you got hurt to keep things moving. They've hung up the sheetrock and we should be painting next week sometime. When you're better, you can do the built-ins we talked about," Cari babbled.

Ray struggled to catch up. "Do you have to go already? We could order takeout and relax before the girls get to your place." Ray wanted more time with her.

"Another time. You should get some rest. You look tired, and remember, you're still healing. I'll be around." Cari pecked his cheek, touched his arm, and slipped out the back door.

Dismayed, he watched her hurry home. Scratching his head, he turned and picked up the coffee pot. "What just happened? One minute we're talking and the next she can't get out of here fast enough." The house felt empty, devoid of warmth. Abruptly, he turned the pot off, grabbed the truck keys off the hook, and headed out the back door. He needed to talk to Jake. He wasn't about to let her walk out the proverbial door.

Chapter Fourteen

"**M**OM, ARE YOU HOME?" Ellie shouted as she walked through the kitchen.

She paused and silence answered her, until she heard a muffled hiccup. Ellie went to the doorway of the semidarkened living room and flipped the lights on. Cari sat with her feet propped up and a mug of cold tea forgotten on the side table.

Confused, Ellie walked over and put the back of her hand gently on Cari's cheek. "Mom?"

Cari glanced at Ellie with tear-filled eyes and attempted to focus on the magazine resting in her lap. Ellie sank down on the arm of the chair and waited for her mother to speak. Cari was not someone who could be rushed. The toot of a car horn could be heard from the driveway. "That's Kate with takeout. I'm going to go help her and I'll be right back. Can I get you anything?"

Cari shook her head no.

Ellie flew to the back door and flung it open. She grabbed a bag from Kate and pulled her inside the house. In a hoarse whisper she said, "Something's terribly wrong with Mom. I found her sitting in the dark. She's been crying. Hurry!" Ellie didn't wait for Kate to get her jacket off before prodding her deeper into the house.

Alarmed, Kate said, "She was fine when she left the shop this afternoon." Kate followed close her sister.

"Mom," Kate said softly, "what are you doing in the dark? Are you sick?" Kate dropped to her knees to look her in the eye.

Cari looked at her daughters. Realizing she was scaring them half to death, she said. "I'm okay. I think the last few months have finally caught up with me and I'm having a momentary meltdown. It's nothing for you two to worry about." She moved to get up from the chair. "I'm glad you girls are here. I think I've picked the perfect color for the room!" Cari said with false bravado.

"I have a better idea, why don't you sit right here and we'll have a picnic on the floor, like we used to when we were little. Kate and I will go get everything and be right back." Ellie gave her mom a tender smile and Kate followed her, looking back over her shoulder as their mom settled into the chair.

"What do you think, Kate?" Ellie was shaken to find her mom crying. "She's our rock, even when Daddy died she was strong and rarely cried in front of us, although I'm sure there was an ocean of tears."

"So much has happened over the last few months. The storm, having to rebuild part of the house, and she started dating. And we both know the dates she's been on have turned out to be huge disappointments. I think the breaking point came when Ray was shot, for which she blames herself. She's overwhelmed and needs our support." Kate rubbed Ellie's shoulders in an attempt to quiet her concern. "We'll have dinner and we can either lift her spirits or let her cry it out." The girls picked up two food-laden trays and went back to their mother.

Time spent laughing and hanging out with her girls had always soothed Cari's nerves. Over dinner, Ellie broached the subject of her coffee date with Al and Cari firmly stated her decision to get off the dating sites.

"I can't believe Al turned out to be a big lying jerk. And then, to ask you for coffee again just to say you're not a match because you're too old. Good riddance, he's a big time loser." Ellie snorted.

Kate jumped in, "Did he really think you wouldn't notice that he was short? Who lies about something that obvious? But when I think back to some of the losers I've dated I guess we all have to kiss a lot of frogs." Kate shook her head.

"So, Mom, what qualities would you look for in a man?" Kate was deliberately baiting her mother, she wanted to get started on Operation Next Door Neighbor.

Cari contemplated confiding in her daughters or evading the question completely. Without looking directly at them, she decided to let the conversation unravel.

"Well, I believe a man should be easy to talk with, have a playful sense of humor and be smart. Good looking never hurts, but it's what's inside that is more important. Oh, and someone who's taller than me, but not too tall."

They all giggled, thinking about Al. "What else?" Ellie prompted her.

Cari got a dreamy faraway look. "Well, hopefully he'd like to garden and putter around the house and spend lots of time together. It won't matter what we're doing as long as we're having fun."

Kate and Ellie sat up a little straighter—something was definitely up with their mom. The girls caught a glimpse of the smile that hovered on her lips.

"Mom, have you met someone?" Kate prodded.

"When have I had time to meet anyone? Things have been slightly hectic around here lately, the gardens, house, shop, and the shooting." Cari saw Kate grinning. "Although there is someone you know and he's a great guy." Cari deliberately let the sentence hang in the air, waiting for the girls to take the bait.

It didn't take but a nanosecond before Ellie demanded, "Are you kidding, don't keep us in suspense! Who is he?"

Before Ellie could pepper Cari with questions, she held up the palm of her hand. "Ray." She was relieved to have it out in the open at last.

"You like him!" Kate teased.

"He's my very good friend." Cari was uncomfortable saying she had the hots for the handsome guy next door.

"But he does have the qualities I think are important in a partner."

"Mom, you're blushing. You do like him. Don't deny it." Ellie giggled.

Kate rubbed her hands together with anticipation. Her plan worked! Her mother finally figured out she had fallen in love with Ray. Well, at least she hoped her mom knew it was love.

Curiosity unleashed, the girls were dying to get the details. "Okay, so has he asked you out on a real date yet?"

"No, he hasn't asked me out and I don't even know if he's interested in me." Cari realized that was the issue—not that she had feelings for Ray but that she didn't know how he felt about her.

"He'd be crazy if he wasn't interested in you. You're beautiful, smart, funny, and a kind and compassionate person," Ellie reassured her. Kate bobbed her head in agreement. Everyone knew by the way Ray looked at her mother he definitely had strong feelings for her. Wisely, Kate wasn't going to spill the beans. Cari needed to discover that for herself.

"So, when did you know that you liked him? Details!" they demanded.

"Honestly, it was the shooting. I didn't think about protecting myself. The only thing I clearly remember was I felt compelled to protect him. Everything happened so fast and then I was holding his head in my lap, waiting for the EMTs. I prayed he wouldn't die. I was talking to him, telling him I was there and I wasn't going anywhere. I was very scared and I kept thinking, what if I lost him? Since then, I've been walking around in a daze, confused. Then today, I stopped over and he wanted to tell me about Vanessa. I hugged him and for that brief moment when we held each other, I felt like I was home. At that moment I knew how I felt and it scared the heck out of me."

The girls interrupted her. "You hugged him? Like how, stuffing coming out of him or just a sweet little ho hum hug?" Kate pried.

Cari ignored her pushy daughter. "A gentle hug. After all, he's been shot and I didn't want to cause him any pain."

"But you wanted to hug the stuffing out of him, didn't you?" Ellie prompted.

"Truth be told, I guess I did, and when I left I kissed him on the cheek and my knees went weak. If kissing him on the cheek made me flustered what would it be like if he really kissed me? Did I mention he smells great?" Cari was serious. It had been a long time since she had a first anything with a man.

"Mom, you need a plan," Kate announced. "Ask him if he wants to have dinner or something—" Cari interrupted Kate by shaking her head.

"I can't do that. I'm old-fashioned. If he's interested, he'll need to ask me out on a date."

"We're in a new millennium, Mom. It's perfectly acceptable for you to ask him. But, if you're not comfortable with dinner then ask him to stop over and see what the boys have done to the room," Ellie suggested.

Cari shook her head. "No, that's not a good idea either. He can stop over whenever he wants."

Kate got up and retrieved Cari's laptop. She handed it to her mom, "Log in to the dating site."

Cari looked at her like she was nuts. "Why would I do that? I don't want to find another date."

"You're going to send Ray a wink, or whatever they call it," Kate suggested. "When he responds, you can start a conversation like you're not sure who he is. When he asks you out for coffee you'll know that he's interested in you."

Cari wasn't so sure about this idea. It sounded a little harebrained but worth a try, and what did she have to lose?

She logged in and did a quick search for Ray profile. "Well, now what do I do? His profile isn't on the site anymore. He must have found someone and doesn't know how to tell me."

"Mom, when has he had time to date? He's been shot and in a hospital," Kate admonished.

"You know what? I'm not going to chase him." The girls had heard the tone in Cari's voice many times in the past, it meant end of discussion. They got the message. Time to move on to a different subject.

"So, about those paint chips?" Kate pulled them from her pocket. "I picked up these little tester bottles so we can paint small section of the walls and try out a few colors. I got one that's your favorite, too, Mom."

Ellie knew what Kate had up her sleeve and they all got up from the floor and went into the sunroom.

Cari flipped on all the lights. The room was as bright as the midday sun. The track lighting had been installed with dimmers to control the level. Cari was excited to see the color choices Kate brought with her. "I think we should paint all these colors, and I'll live with them for a couple of days to see what works best."

β β β β β β β β

Ray arrived at Jake's just as he and Sara got home from work. Sara insisted he stay for dinner. Ray nursed a beer that Jake had set in front of him. He was clueless how to broach the subject of Cari with his son.

Jake waited for his father to stop stewing. History told him to be patient.

The two men sat in silence for a while until Ray said, "Jake? What do you think if I said I wanted to get serious with a woman?" Ray sheepishly looked at his son, hoping for the best.

"Dad, you don't need my permission to date, and we'd say it's about time! You should get out there, have some fun, travel, and do whatever. You've worked hard and deserve to enjoy life. When you find her, I know we'll love her as much as you do," Jake teased.

Sara was listening as she stayed busy in the kitchen. "Do you have someone special in mind or is this a 'what if' kind of question?" She prayed he'd say what they suspected to be true about Cari McKenna.

"Well, there is a woman I've been thinking about asking out for dinner, but I wasn't sure if it would be too weird. And now she's doing this stupid Internet dating thing and it's driving me half crazy." Ray's frustration was apparent.

Sara crossed the short space and sat next to Ray. Taking his hand, she said, "I couldn't love you anymore than if you were my own dad and it bothers me that you're sitting here asking us for permission to date Cari."

Shock crossed his face and his cheeks flushed to a deep shade of crimson. "What makes you think it's Cari?"

Suppressing a giggle, Sara continued, "Please. A blind person can see what's written all over your face, you're smitten with her. You light up when she's around!"

"People must think I'm some kind of fool mooning over a woman at my age."

"You're not old and have nothing to be embarrassed about. She's a terrific person who, I'm pretty sure, has feelings for you. Apparently it's taking her some time to figure it out, too." Sara studied his face. "Why do you think she would have put herself between you and a loaded gun?" Sara squeezed his hand to encourage confidence.

Jake interjected, "Dad, I'm not a little kid anymore. I want you have someone to share your life with. If I could pick someone for you, Cari would be my only choice. She's a great mom, business owner, and friend, and I think she'd make a terrific partner for you. You've dated over the years but you've never found anyone that makes you smile like she does. Dad, open your eyes, see who's been in front of you all these years. If you did, you wouldn't be sitting here asking our permission. Do all of us a favor and just ask her to have dinner, and soon."

Ray listened to the kids. It was simple; they wanted him to be happy.

Puzzled, he asked, "Exactly what do you mean by 'all of us'?"

"Relax, Dad. Sara and I have talked with Cari's kids about this for the last couple of years. We're your biggest fans. And I would finally have siblings. How great would that be?" Jake beamed.

Ray was still puzzled. "Why haven't you ever said anything?"

"Hey, it's not our place to tell you how to live your life. With enough time, we were hoping you'd figure it out. And here you are, figuring it out." Jake clapped his hand on his dad's shoulder, momentarily forgetting that a few days ago he had been in the hospital recovering from surgery.

Sara gave Ray a hug and pecked his cheek. "If you need any advice where to take Cari, let me know. I'm a phone call away."

Later that night Ray was sitting on his deck, gazing out over the backyard, and mulling over his son's advice. Stunned didn't begin to cover what he felt when Sara told him it was about time he got around to asking Cari out on an official date. The lights came on in Cari's sunroom. Ray took it as a sign. "Time waits for no man," he muttering as he dialed her number.

The phone ringing interrupted Cari midsentence. She glanced at her watch. Who could be calling now? She held up a finger to the girls to keep their chatter quiet for a minute.

"Hello?"

"Cari, did I catch you at a bad time?"

"Hi, Ray. No, the girls and I are hanging out, looking at paint colors. Is everything okay?"

"Getting better every minute," His voice was strong and clear. "Um, I was wondering, if you're not busy, would you like to have dinner with me tomorrow night? I thought we could try the new Thai place in town. Or, if you're busy, maybe another night soon?" Silently Ray reminded himself to keep his voice steady. Who would have thought at his age he would be nervous to ask a woman for a date?

Surprised, Cari sank onto an upside-down crate. "I'd like that. I've wanted to try it and I've heard the food is excellent."

"I'll pick you up at half past six, if that gives you enough time?" Ray hoped he could wait that long.

"Perfect, I'll look forward to it. See you tomorrow." Cari hung up the phone and turned to the girls.

In unison Kate and Ellie asked, "Mom? Was that Ray?"

Cari slowly nodded her head. "He asked me to have dinner with him tomorrow night. Why do you suppose that is?" Cari had come to terms with the notion that she was interested in him and now he had called and invited her to dinner.

"Maybe he wants to thank you for saving his life," Ellie suggested.

"Or maybe he wants to have dinner with a gorgeous woman instead of eating the casserole she left for him," Kate interjected.

"Or maybe he wants to tell me that since he had this life-threatening event he's decided we can't spend so much time together because he's found someone else." Cari went from excited to doubtful she would enjoy the evening.

"You don't know that. Seriously, I doubt he would ask you to have dinner just to tell you he found someone else. No guy asks a girl to dinner just to say they're going to be friends."

"Yeah, there isn't anyone that would make him as happy as you can. So think positive," Ellie chimed in.

"Forget about paint colors," Kate said, "We need to go upstairs and pick out an outfit that will be guaranteed to knock his socks off." Kate and Ellie each grabbed a hand and pulled her off the crate. "Come on, let's see what you've got, and, if you don't have anything nice to wear, we're shopping in the morning. This is quite a turn of events."

Cari's mind raced. What would she tell Ray when he broke his news? That she was happy for him and he deserved all the happiness in the world? Of course she would, and hopefully they could be friends as well as neighbors. Pleased with her plan, she happily succumbed to the girls rifling through her closet.

"Pixie, since we recently dug through the closet I don't think there is anything new to choose from. Let's pick something classy." From the expression on her mom's face, she could tell it was whirling with a million different thoughts. Kate was willing to bet that after tomorrow night Cari would have a different reason to whirl.

Kate stood in front of the open closet. Slowly sliding hangers, she scrutinized the options. "Mom has great legs and she should show them off. She's beautiful and, by gosh, she's going to look the part tomorrow night!"

Kate looked over her shoulder at her mom. "Don't worry you're going to look gorgeous Mom. Ellie, come help, she's got to have something that will transform her from coffee lady to a heart-stopping date."

Cari wondered if she'd survive the night. Happier than she had been in a long time, she stood up. "Okay, dress me." Laughter rang out as clothes flew from the closet.

Chapter Fifteen

CARI FELT LIKE A WOMAN GETTING READY FOR HER FIRST DATE. She dressed in a deep green, A-line, midcalf length dress with a modest scoop neckline. Silver twisted hoops graced her ears and her dark hair hung in loose waves around her shoulders. She slipped a long silver necklace over her head. Beads in various shades of green, pink, and lavender reflected the light. Dark brown boots and a suede jacket completed the look.

Glancing in the mirror, she double-checked her make-up. Nerves jangling she strained to hear tires crunch in the driveway. She didn't want to keep Ray waiting. As soon as she heard his truck, she tucked her keys inside the handbag and pulled the door firmly shut behind her.

Ray got out of his truck and stopped dead in his tracks. He couldn't remember when Cari had looked more beautiful.

Cari caught the look on his face, pleased that the time she spent pulling together her outfit had paid off. From under her lashes, she stole a look at her date. He was handsome in black jeans and a frosty blue button-down shirt—which made his blue eyes brighter than usual—and a gray herringbone jacket. His high cheekbones flushed with color beneath his tan. The butterflies in her stomach went wild. Ray gently steered her to the passenger side, holding the door open for her. Cari settled in the seat for the short drive to the restaurant.

At a loss for words, Cari struggled to find something to talk about. "How are you feeling today? Did you sleep well last night? Sleeping at home has to be better than in the hospital where they are poking you all night. And with the noise in that place, I'm surprised anyone gets any rest." Cari inhaled a shaky breath, realizing she was doing a decent job covering up a bad case of nerves.

Amused, Ray waited patiently for her to take a breath so he could respond to even one of her questions. He had his opening. "I'm feeling much better, and you are right, I think you always sleep best in your own bed."

When he smiled and she was reminded this was Ray, a man she had been friends with for years, she began to relax and enjoy their evening.

Ray was positive that if he didn't have a steering wheel to grip, his hands would be shaking like a leaf. He stopped talking to concentrate on driving.

"I haven't been to this new restaurant and I'm not sure what it's called." Ray peered through the windshield, looking at storefronts. "Siam, that's simple and to the point." He grinned. "There's a parking place up a block, is that okay?"

"Sure, after we eat we may need to stretch our legs."

Ray put the truck in park and Cari reached for the door handle.

"Hold on, I'll get that for you."

Ray quickly crossed in front of the truck. Holding the door open, he offered his hand, helping her out of the vehicle. His fingers grazed hers, sending a pleasant sensation through his body. Touching her wasn't doing anything to help steady his nerves.

Inside the restaurant, the hostess escorted them to a cozy table tucked in a back corner. It was quiet and a good place for private conversation. The waitress promptly came to take their drink order and drifted away, leaving Ray and Cari alone.

At a loss for words, Cari sat with her hands folded in her lap, unsure what she should say or do next.

Ray cleared his throat and she thought, Oh no, he's getting it over with before dinner. She braced herself, waiting for the inevitable words to come out of his mouth.

"Cari," Ray began softly, looking deep into her emerald eyes. "We've been spending a great deal of time together over the last several of months. I've had fun with you. I've enjoyed the conversations we've had and working with you to rebuild your home. Time spent with you flies by. I find myself drawn to your sense of humor, kindness, and your willingness to try anything and everything, but most of all your generous spirit. I love being with you and I have never felt like this with another person."

Cari started to interrupt, but Ray held up his hand. "Please just another minute."

Cari sat in the chair, dumbfounded.

"I might not be what you had in mind when you posted your profile online, but when I looked at yours it confirmed what I've felt for a long time. You know me, Cari, and I know you. We've been neighbors for years and we've both seen more than our fair share of heartache, with Ben's death, being single parents, and my divorce. We have many other things in common. Also, we have a solid friendship of many years. I'd like to ask you if you'd do me the honor of dating me."

Cari sat, unable to articulate a single word. Ray looked away, embarrassed at the silence that hung in the air. He didn't expect her to fall into his arms but he had hoped she'd say something, laugh at him, or maybe even tell him he was crazy. But now he felt like the biggest jerk in town.

Cari choked back tears. "Ray, are you sure you want to date me? I was convinced you wanted to bring me here tonight to tell me that you'd met someone and we won't be able to spend time together." Relief coursed through her. Cari didn't know what to do first, laugh or cry. Laughing, she said, "I see that was exactly what you did except the woman is me."

Encouraged, he reached over to take her hands in his. "Cari, didn't you see this coming? I've cared for you for a very long time. According to our kids, my feelings are written on my face. I don't know what I've been waiting for but getting shot put things in perspective. It hit me when I was flat on my back in critical care. Life only comes around once. We don't get do-overs. When you signed up for Internet dating, I was a mess. Selfishly, I wished it could be me waiting for you in the coffee shop or wherever you went to meet someone."

Cari grinned at him, caressing his hands, happiness flooding her heart.

"What do you say? Can we see where this road will take us?" Ray finished his carefully rehearsed speech. He caught the waitress in the corner of his eye waiting for a signal to deliver the drinks. Ray nodded, giving Cari time to gather her thoughts.

Cari couldn't contain herself. "Ray, I can't believe you have felt like this and I never knew. I wish you had said something long ago. Maybe the time wasn't right and we weren't ready. I don't need to think about it, we need to give 'us' a chance."

Cautiously, Ray said, "So, can we call this our first official date?"

Cari gave him a smile that would light up the midnight sky. "Yes, this is our first official date! I don't know about you but I'm starved. Do you think our waitress will bring our dinner out soon?"

Not being able to control himself, Ray let out a deep belly laugh, grabbed his stomach, and kept laughing. "God, that hurts, but it feels so good."

Ray gave a silent thanks to their kids. When did they get smarter than their parents? He sat back and savored each moment with Cari.

After a leisurely dinner, they strolled down Main Street in the crisp air. The sky was dotted with a million stars. Cari tucked her hands around Ray's arm, resting her head against his shoulder.

The park was deserted and they had their choice of benches. The park lamps softly illuminated the footpaths.

They sat on a bench that faced Cari's shop and Main Street. Conversation was easy and they found themselves talking about the kids.

"Can you believe they had this figured out a long time ago?"

"How could they have known when we didn't know ourselves?" he said.

"If Kate thought we were interested in each other, why on earth did she encourage me to sign up for online dating?" she wondered.

"Well, I don't know why she encouraged you but I can tell you I was jealous. I wanted you to be happy and have someone in your life but when you started dating, I was lost. I would have given anything to meet you for coffee, and I wouldn't have been late." Ray pulled her a little tighter in his arms. Now that he had her, he wasn't letting go.

Suddenly she sat straight up. "I know what that little minx was up to!" she exclaimed. "She knew if I started dating you'd get jealous or I'd get sick of the losers and eventually we would start dating. Her assumption was that at some point we would realize what we had been missing all this time." Cari started to laugh. "Well, she was right. I did get sick of it and it sounds like she had you pegged, too."

"I thought that same thing just an hour or so ago." Ray pulled her back into his arms, breathing in her floral perfume.

Cari sighed, content in Ray's arms until the cold penetrated their bliss.

"Maybe we should call it a night," Ray suggested.

Cari didn't want the night to end but Ray needed rest and she had a shop to run. He stood up and held out his hand for her. They strolled hand in hand to the truck.

On the drive home, Cari was nervous. What would he expect when they got back to her house? Should she invite him in or give him a quick hug good-bye. It had been a long time since she had an old-fashioned first date.

She glanced at Ray. She couldn't read the look on his face but she was sure they both had fun.

They pulled into the driveway. Cari knew one of them had to say something. She summoned up her courage and cleared her throat. "I had a wonderful time tonight and I am excited to see where our friendship goes. I hope you understand what I'm going to say next. I've been alone a long time and you know I haven't dated, well except for the recent disasters. Would it be okay if we took things slow?" Cari didn't want to offend him but she wasn't comfortable with the idea of a physical relationship, at least not yet.

"We don't need to rush into anything, Cari. We'll go as slow as you want and let nature take its course. There aren't any rules we have to follow."

Ray understood exactly where she was coming from and he wasn't going to push her and screw this up. He knew he would spend the rest of his life with this woman. Cari wasn't ready to hear that bit of news. It would scare the heck out of her. Luckily, patience was his middle name.

Ray reached over to take her hand. He gave it a little squeeze, reassuring her that he was okay with a slower pace. "Let me walk you to the door, you're cold."

He reached over to push the door open and by the time he made his way around to the other side she was standing next to it, smoothing down the front of her dress. They walked to the door and awkwardly stood in the glow of the front porch light, neither of them sure what to do next.

Cari broke the ice. "Is it okay if I hug you?"

Grateful she made the first move, he said, "Of course it is." He opened his arms and she stepped into the circle of his warmth, inhaling his musky aftershave.

"You smell yummy," Cari mumbled into his chest.

He had longed to hold her in his arms and he could scarcely believe it was happening. He placed a soft kiss on the top of her head as she slowly pulled away from him with a slight shiver.

"I had a wonderful time tonight, thank you," Cari said shyly.

"You don't have to thank me for having fun, Cari."

"I'll stop by tomorrow at the coffee shop. But don't worry if I'm not there early, I may sleep late, if I can." Ray leaned in and placed a chaste kiss on Cari's cheek. "Good night, Cari. Sleep well."

Cari turned to unlock the door and hesitated for a moment, turning to look back over her shoulder at Ray.

"Good night and sweet dreams!" she said softly, went inside, and closed the door behind her.

He stood on her doorstep gazing like a love-struck teenager at the door. Reluctantly, he turned to go home. He was counting the hours until he could see her again. It felt good to be alive.

Cari leaned against the door, waiting for the shakiness in her knees to subside. The evening had turned out better than she had dreamed. Wait until she got her hands on her girls, especially Kate. What were they thinking, encouraging her to sign up for Internet dating? Restless, she wandered through the dimly lit house, finding her way into the semi-finished sunroom. Her piano stood in the corner, patiently waiting for her to have the desire to play. The keys had been silent since the night of the storm. For the first time in weeks, the music called to her, allowing her to express what she didn't completely understand. She slid gracefully onto the bench, coming to rest in the center of the keyboard. A few tentative notes floated on the air. She ran her long fingers over the keys with familiarity, warming them up. Readjusting her hands, she let the melodic tones seep from her fingers. She played without thought, lost in the emotion of the music as it wrapped her in a familiar embrace. She was unaware the music that poured from her fingers was a window to her innermost thoughts.

Ray was walking to his back door but stopped midstep when the first notes reached him. He could picture Cari sitting in front of her piano. The music was happy, light, and romantic, it caressed his heart. Content that she was playing tonight, he turned and went inside the house.

Cari played for hours, lost in the pleasure of her music. The music dipped into a quiet section and she heard him behind her, "This is one of the things I miss most, the way you play."

Her fingers hovered midnote over the keys, caught between the desire to keep playing for him or turn and talk to him.

She kept playing. "I'm surprised you're here tonight. I didn't expect to see you again after you told me I had to move on with my life."

"Cari, you knew I would have come at least one more time," Ben said quietly. "We are connected in a way that most people never find—a connection that wasn't broken by death. There is an invisible silken thread reaching between here to the heavens."

"Oh, Ben, I'm happy you're here. I've thought about what you said and I had a long talk with Kate. You would be so proud of her! She's grown into a lovely young woman." Cari laughed. "Her husband, Donovan, is quiet, strong and easy going, in some ways very much like you. He is the perfect complement for her Irish temper. It took him a while to convince her to have dinner, but persistence paid off and after the first date she was hooked. At first I was worried, she was so young, but they're two peas in a pod."

Cari grew quiet. "Why did you come back tonight?"

"I watch over them and I know they're doing well," Ben reassured her. "Just as I have always watched over you." Ben smiled at his beautiful girl. "I must confess you've worried me from time to time, but standing in front of a loaded gun? I'm proud that you saved Ray's life. You have always been very brave. I'm happy you've opened your heart to him and that you're ready to accept what he has to offer you. I was beginning to think I'd never become a memory."

Ben chuckled when a look of annoyance flickered over Cari's features. "I specifically chose tonight to come here because you're ready for me to be your past. And the thought of missing me won't overwhelm you. You won't need me to talk with you about problems with the kids or your business."

Tears ran unchecked down her cheeks. "I have never stopped loving you, not for one second. How I feel about Ray doesn't change anything that we had." Cari felt this might be the last time she would talk to Ben and she had to make it count.

"Sweetheart, I know that. I've always felt well loved. But physically I can't be with you. We're both ready for you to move on. If you ever need me, remember our life together and that's where I'll be. Love doesn't die, Cari, people do." Cari blinked away her tears to see him clearly.

"Cari, we loved each other deeply. Your heart has found someone who will love you like no one else on earth can. Revel in the glow of his love. Let yourself be open to accept what he has to offer you, things that you can't have living with the memory of me. Life has a way of giving you what you need exactly when you're ready for it. For many years, you needed me, and I came to you. You weren't ready to let go but now it's time." His eyes held hers captive. "Cari, I will love you for all eternity."

"Ben!" she cried. It was too late. He was gone. "I love you." She whispered into the night.

Cari sat on the piano bench, listening to the sounds of her home. For the first time in twenty-five-plus years, it felt empty. Ben was gone. The clock struck twice, it was early morning, and she was surprised at how quickly the night had evaporated. She was drained and tired but not ready to sleep. Wondering if Ellie would be awake, Cari dialed her cell, half expecting voicemail to pick up.

Ellie glanced at her phone. It was her mother. Concerned, she picked up. "Hi, Mom, what's up?"

"Everything is fine, Pixie. I wanted to hear your voice. The house seems empty tonight without you here. Did I wake you up or interrupt you studying?" Cari spoke in a hushed voice.

"No, I was doing a little studying, nothing important. I decided to stay at the dorm because I have an early class but if you want I can come home, we can make hot cocoa and have girl talk." Ellie wasn't sure what was going on. It was out of character for her mother to call so late. "I can hop in the car and be there in a jiff."

Already feeling better, she chided, "Don't be silly, I'm fine. I wanted to tell you about my date with Ray. You and your sister were right. He has feelings for me and has for a long time! Here I was, worried he wanted to tell me that he had found someone. Well, he did and it's me." Cari giggled like a schoolgirl remembering the exact moment it hit her that she was the woman he wanted.

"That's wonderful. I hate to say it but we told you there wasn't anything to worry about. Did you call Kate and tell her the good news?" Ellie asked. "Or Shane?"

"Actually, you're the first person I called. I didn't want to wake up Kate. You know she goes to bed early and I'm not sure Shane really wants an update on my love life." Cari was chuckling, thinking of what Shane would say if she had called him.

Ellie sighed in relief. "I'll stop by the shop in the morning and we can have a late breakfast together. You can fill Kate and me in on all the juicy details. But wait for me to get there, don't tell Kate first. It will be like the old days when Kate would get home, you would make us late-night chocolate chip pancakes, and we'd dissect her date." Ellie quickly warmed up to the idea. "But remember don't give Kate any details before I get there, alright? And to be absolutely clear, we don't want to hear about anything unless it's G-rated." Ellie cracked up.

"Not to worry, kiddo, I don't kiss and tell." Cari's mood had lightened considerably since she had dialed Ellie's number. "I'm going to let you go so you can get some sleep. Remember, the first rule for looking your best is plenty of rest. I'm going to send Grace a text and see if she wants to join us. I'm sure she won't want to miss the breaking news."

"Even better idea. See you in the morning. Mom, I love you. I'm glad you a good time tonight." Ellie clicked off the line.

Cari hung up the phone and one by one turned off the lights as she made her way upstairs. She hoped sleep would come quickly. She couldn't wait to see Ray tomorrow.

Chapter Sixteen

R AY WOKE AND ROLLED OVER TO GLANCE AT THE CLOCK, surprised to find it was late morning. Grinning, he hopped out of bed and buzzed through the shower, anxious to get down to Cari's shop. The night before had been amazing and he planned to play hooky with his girl. He hoped Kate would pitch in and cover Cari for a while.

ᦤ ᦤ ᦤ ᦤ ᦤ ᦤ ᦤ ᦤ

Cari sat at a small table overflowing with dishes. Grace and the girls were finishing the last plate of pancakes. The only thing that saved her from getting hammered with questions when they walked through the door was that food always came first for these girls.

Cari watched as Grace pushed sliced fruit around her plate, impatiently waiting to find out what the heck was going on. The last time Cari had talked with Grace she announced she was done with Internet dating. Grace took a sip of herbal tea and smiled at her friend, observing the new glow her GF wore.

"Let's clear the dirty dishes and get recaffeinated and then we can hear the nitty-gritty details about last night," Kate said, giving Cari a case of nervous giggles.

"Well? What's going on with your hunk?" Grace demanded good-naturedly. "You've kept us in suspense long enough. I got your text saying you had big news, that you had met a man. I expected a follow-up message with details, but what did I get? Silence. Well, I take that back, you asked me to come for breakfast. So, do I know who he is? Spill it."

"As a matter of fact you do know him!" Cari paused, letting the suspense build.

Grace and Kate and Ellie grinned like Cheshire cats, hoping they knew what she was about to say.

"Ray!" she gushed.

Cari was radiant. The door jingled as Sara came in. The ladies turned to greet her.

"Can anyone join the party?" Sara smiled.

Cari got up to give her a hug and pulled up a chair for her. "Of course you can. I was wondering if we'd see you today. I hear that you had a hand in recent events," Cari prodded.

"It depends on what happened. If you're talking about Ray, he came to see us a couple of days ago and he was in a lather, asking Jake if he could get seriously involved with someone. Ray was beating around the bush so we told him to ask you out, and we also told him all of us were wondering what was taking the two of you so long to get together." The girls nodded as Sara told the story.

Cari was dumbfounded. "I had a similar conversation with Kate and Ellie. Great minds think alike, I guess."

"So . . . Mom," Ellie teased, "tell all, and remember keep it G-rated, please."

"Details, Cari. You're not allowed to leave out one single tidbit so start at the beginning!" Grace wanted to savor the romantic details of her friend's first date. "Charlie and I have been married forever and I don't remember what the first blush of romance was like. My sweet husband is romantic but there wasn't anything like the first few months of new love." Grace let out an audible sigh, making everyone laugh.

"Well, to bring everybody up to speed, Ray asked me to have dinner and I was sure he wanted to tell me he had met someone. I was prepared to hear that we wouldn't be able to spend as much time together. I'm not sure if you all know, but we have been spending some time together, impromptu drinks or dinner over the last few months," Cari stated.

"You were? How come you never told us?" Ellie demanded.

"I didn't think it was that big of a deal. After all, friends can have dinner together. When I've had dinner with Grace I didn't tell you both," Cari said defensively.

"No offense, Grace, but you aren't a dark-haired, blue-eyed guy from next door," Kate said.

"None taken!" Grace smirked.

Letting the comment pass, Cari was still defensive. "I don't think I need to ask permission about who I chose to spend time with." Cari went to get the coffee pot. Standing, poised to pour, she continued, "Do you want to hear the rest of the story or not?"

Ellie bobbed her head. "Go on."

"We went to the new Thai place up the street. The food was good, too." Cari started drifting off topic.

"Mom, we don't care about the food." Kate gently redirected her mom.

Cari smiled. "He told me I looked nice but I think he was kind of surprised to see me wearing a dress. Whether it's here or home I'm in jeans and T-shirts. Oh, and he looked amazing!" She tilted her head back and laid her hands across her heart.

She exhaled. "Where was I? Okay, to start with, I was very nervous and started babbling to fill the awkward silence in the truck. Thank heavens it is a short drive into town. We get to the restaurant, and he held the doors open for me, can you believe that? Anyway, we order but before the drinks arrive, he starts talking about how he feels about me and that he wants to get to know me as more than just a friend. Of course, I was in total shock and at a loss for words, which made him think I wasn't interested. You know he's a man of few words, so I had to jump in, and fast, to tell him I wanted to date him, too. Then he said the sweetest thing, he wished he could have met me for a coffee date instead of the jerks that I've had to deal with." Cari looked around the table to see four sets of misty eyes watching her, hanging on every word.

Grace broke the silence. "Cari, there isn't anyone I know that deserves happiness more than you. Ray is a very lucky guy."

Sara quickly agreed and grabbed Cari's hand to give it a reassuring squeeze. "Jake and I have been praying that Dad would finally see you as more than simply his friend and neighbor. We couldn't be happier."

Kate and Ellie closely observed their mother. She had blossomed overnight.

"Katie, you are awfully quiet." Cari was concerned.

"Mom, it's about time! I thought I was going to have to dress Ray up in neon or something for you to notice him. Oh, and for the record, Don and Shane feel exactly the same way as the rest of us!" Kate grinned so big it looked like her cheeks might split.

"This calls for a celebration!" Kate jumped up but stopped short as Ray walked in.

Giggling, the ladies started moving around the shop, picking up dirty dishes, straightening chairs, or whatever they could do to give some semblance of privacy to Ray and Cari.

Ray looked around. "I feel like I'm interrupting something pretty important?"

"No, of course not. The girls and Grace were enjoying a late breakfast and Sara stopped by for coffee."

Based on the reaction when he walked in, Ray suspected he had been the topic of conversation.

"Any chance I could get a late breakfast or an early lunch?" he said hopefully. "I overslept and I don't have much in the way of food at my house except for remnants of a delicious casserole that I've eaten at every meal for days."

"I don't know what I was thinking. I should have picked up a few groceries for you when you came home. What would you like? I have chocolate chip pancake batter. That's what we had. Maybe a couple of scrambled eggs and bacon to go with them?" Cari moved toward the kitchen.

"You had chocolate chip pancakes for breakfast?" Pretending to be shocked, he teased, "What happened to 'a healthy breakfast is essential to start the day'?"

"It's a long and very old story that I'll tell you some-time. But for now what would you like?"

"You know chocolate chip pancakes would hit the spot. A couple of eggs and bacon, too. I'm starving!"

"I'm adding sliced bananas, too!" Cari joked.

Ray trailed behind her, making his way into the kitchen. "May I get some coffee?" he asked no one in particular.

"Help yourself!" Ellie yelled from the walk-in fridge. "Then pop a squat and we'll bring out some hot pancakes shortly."

All thoughts of stealing a couple of minutes with Cari quickly vanished. The party had relocated to the kitchen in hopes of continuing their conversation. Reversing his direc-tion, Ray took a seat at a table with a clear line of sight of the front counter. He wasn't expecting Cari to sit down while he had breakfast but he was pleased when she came strolling over with a fresh mug of coffee.

"Would you like some company?" she asked with a shy smile.

"Absolutely!" Ray hastily pulled out a chair for her. "I was wondering if you could slip out early today. I'd like to check out the sunroom and see what the boys have accom-plished. I'm frustrated all I can do is oversee the installers and maybe get Jake to help me with the cabinets."

"You're going to be pleased to see their progress. Let me check with Kate. I'm sure she won't mind, and maybe Grace has time to cover the front."

Cari glided across the shop, comfortable in her surroundings. An exchange of female voices murmuring emanated from the kitchen. Smiling, Cari joined him again, Grace on her heels taking up a position behind the counter.

"Good news, I'm free as a bird. As soon as you're done eating, we can take off. We should stop at the market and pick up a few things for your house." Cari's eyes sparkled. "I like the idea of playing hooky. So eat up."

Ray didn't need to be told twice. He inhaled the last of his breakfast and washed it down with a gulp of coffee. He didn't need a refill or a to-go cup, his energy level skyrocketed as soon as Cari agreed to spend the day with him.

Cari grabbed her coat and bag, waving as they walked out the door. She could feel Grace and the girls smirking, knowing they ran to the window to watch the couple stroll down the street. Oblivious to their audience, Ray clasped Cari's hand in his.

⋐ ⋐ ⋐ ⋐ ⋐ ⋐ ⋐ ⋐

Ray pulled in behind Cari at the market. This was a first; Ray had never seen Cari grocery shop. She quickly moved through the produce aisle picking up fruit, smelling and squeezing it to see what was fresh, juicy, and ripe. She inspected vegetables, moved to the fish counter, and then to the bakery for some fresh bread. It didn't take Cari long to make short work of the store.

Standing in the check-out line, Ray was astonished, "Who do you think is going to eat all that food?"

"You are. You have tissue and muscles to repair and you're not going to do that by eating junk food." Cari was on top of the world, nothing could dampen her spirit today. "I got fish for dinner, if you'd like to join me?" she said teasingly.

"I thought you'd never ask." Dinner was an unexpected bonus to the day.

Cari pushed the cart out to the car and began loading the groceries into her trunk.

"I'm not an invalid," Ray said and reached for a bag.

"You have staples holding you together. You need to avoid putting unnecessary stress on them. You can carry all the bags next time." She laid her hand on his arm and brushed past him, stashing the cart in the corral.

"Ready? You have a lot to see at the house." Cari gave him a playful shove toward his truck.

After a quick stop at Ray's to drop off his car, he got into Cari's car for the short ride to her place. "The boys have been pretty busy. They make a good team."

Ray allowed himself to be led inside. Upon first glance, he saw it was much closer to completion than he had thought.

"The boys did a great job finishing the sheetrock; the seams look good." He walked over to study the colors painted on the wall. Pointing to them, he asked, "Do you have a favorite?"

"I'm leaning toward the deep taupe, which has a pink undertone. I think it will go well with the floral prints, and it won't dominate the room. It will soften the light if I have the drapes open. If I painted the room off-white, which was my first thought, the room will have that sterile look, and I'm going for warm and inviting."

Cari watched Ray move around the room, carefully inspecting every inch. "I have a confession to make. When you first showed me the renovation plans I wasn't so sure about the drastic changes you suggested—opening up the floor plan and adding more windows. I had gotten used to everything being in the shadows. But now that it's almost done, I can honestly say it's perfect! I'm going to love throwing the doors open in the summer and having the scent of flowers drift inside. I was thinking of adding pots of climbing jasmine—they're beautiful and smell heavenly. The deck will be wonderful to sit and relax with a glass of wine or something. I can't believe I'm about to say this but I think the best thing that's happened to me in a long time was that old tree falling on my house."

Ray stood staring at this woman who had without a second thought trusted him with her home. This was the first time he heard she had been nervous about the changes he suggested to her sanctuary.

"Cari, I'm glad you're happy." Ray gestured to the space. "I had the basic idea but you took it and made subtle changes to reflect your personality. I'm sorry it's not finished yet."

Cari reached out and touched his cheek. "Don't be silly. It will be finished in time for Thanksgiving or Christmas if the electrician shows up," she joked. "I'm happy I can play my piano again."

Ray smiled. "I heard you playing last night. It was beautiful. My turn to confess. Over the years I have spent many nights sitting in my backyard stargazing as you played. I imagined it was a concert just for me." Ray smiled. "You could play a little more rock and roll but I've come to appreciate the classical stuff."

Embarrassed, Cari said, "I had no idea anyone was listening to me. I'm glad you enjoyed me beating on the keys. It's my way of working out problems or issues."

"I know. I could always tell when the kids were pressing on your last nerve or when you were worried about things. You play what you feel."

"Ray, have you been spying on me all these years?" Annoyed, Cari felt he had invaded her private space. Music was her therapy.

Ray was surprised to see her temper flare. "Cari, I wasn't spying on you, I'd never do that. The first time I heard you play was totally by accident, honestly." He wished he hadn't said anything. "After Vanessa left I was lost, being a single parent and wondering what I had done wrong. At night, I would sit and gaze into the darkness to relax. One night, when Jake and I been locking horns I was watching the shooting stars, and you started to play something that was so sad. It felt like you knew exactly how I was feeling, and it was salve for my open wounds. It wasn't anything I did on purpose, it just happened. That night I listened until you stopped playing. Over the years, I got into the habit of stargazing and being your unseen audience. I never told anyone, not even Jake. So many nights your mood matched mine and I have a feeling we worked through a lot of problems together all those nights."

Ray hung his head. "Cari, I would never have invaded your privacy."

An oppressive silence hung in the air. It was time for Ray to leave and not look back. Without another word, he turned and walked out onto the deck.

"Hey! Where do you think you're going? You just got here!" Cari shouted after him. "You can't tell someone you've been listening to them play music for thousands of nights and then walk away like it's no big deal!"

"Cari, I get it and I understand you're mad. Your music soothed my soul and healed my heart. You didn't realize it but you helped me get through the worst time in my life at the same time you were going through hell."

"Ray, I'm flattered. My taste runs to the eclectic. Jazz, rock, country, and throw in a little Beethoven to mix things up and whatever else tickles my fancy." Cari smiled. "I'm sorry I flipped out. When Ben was alive, he used to sit in the sunroom and listen to me play. He always said I always knew exactly what he needed to hear and he found it soothing, too. I guess it threw me for a loop."

Ray opened his arms and she walked into them. They held each other close, hesitant to let go. Cari looked at Ray through her dark lashes. She longed to be kissed but doubts filled her head. What if she was a terrible kisser and their first kiss was their last?

Mesmerized by her emerald eyes, he lowered his lips to hers and placed a chaste kiss on her full, inviting mouth. Ray didn't want to rush her but he couldn't wait another moment, he was dying to melt into her. The first kiss deepened, lasting longer and feeling more satisfying than he'd dreamed.

The kiss stirred feelings Cari thought were long dormant. Without missing a beat, she let him guide her to the couch. She sighed, sinking deeper into his arms.

After several minutes, Cari pulled away from Ray, taking deep gulps of air. Flustered she needed to regain control over what was quickly getting out of hand. "So, do you want to see the flooring samples?"

Ray found Cari charming while her cheeks tinged pink. "Sure, let's see what you chose," he said, basking in the heat of their kiss. He needed a few moments to regain control, too. Discovering how badly he needed her, he also understood the need to move slowly. But after her response, he knew she would be worth the wait.

Chapter Seventeen

T HE WEEKS FLEW BY AS RAY COURTED CARI. It was important to him he respect her wishes and take their budding romance slow. Holding hands, they walked in the autumn leaves, had dinner together almost every night, and spent hours talking about everything. They shared the joy of discovering all the subtle nuances about the other. Ray surprised Cari with his cooking ability, grilling and making his Italian specialty, lasagna.

The foundation of their romance was based on their long-term friendship but the intimate relationship was still new. Ray understood Cari was nervous about their physical relationship. She had been honest, telling Ray she hadn't been involved with anyone since Ben.

Cari looked at her backside in the three-way mirror. There was no denying the truth: her butt had gone south and there wasn't anything she could do to change that fact. She had given birth to a set of twins and then a third child and there had been many candles blown out on birthday cakes. She studied her reflection. "Well, it is what it is." She turned away from the mirror and ran a brush through her hair. She needed to get down to the shop and help Kate. They had committed to providing baked rolls and a pie for her favorite charity, Helping Hands Baskets. There was a lot to get done before they were scheduled to start delivery.

Ten years ago, Grace and Cari heard about a family in need and they put together a basket of food and other necessities to give them a hand. Over the years, it evolved into an annual family event. Each year Cari would be told about families in need. Grace canvased local businesses to donate money, food, and other items. A few days before Thanksgiving, a group of family and close friends gathered at the shop to fill the baskets. The day before Thanksgiving Cari and her kids delivered the baskets. Unfortunately, each year the number of people in need grew. Thankfully, every year the group of volunteers grew in numbers too.

After the basket distribution, Cari hosted a large traditional Thanksgiving dinner. Grace, Charlie, Ray, Jake, and Sara would be joining the McKennas this year. She hoped this would be the first of many holidays they would all spend together.

The phone started to ring as Cari was stepping out the door. Tempted to ignore it, she picked it up. She didn't have time to return the call later. There was too much to get done before the holiday and the shop was hopping with orders.

"Hello," she said over the sound of papers rustling on the other end.

"May I please speak with Mrs. Cari McKenna?" a female voice inquired.

"Speaking." Cari didn't recognize the caller's voice. "Who is this, please?"

"Mrs. McKenna, my name is Holly Jones. I am the paralegal for the attorney representing Vanessa Davis Fisher. I was asked to call you on behalf of Mrs. Fisher. She has requested to see you before her sentencing next week."

Cari gripped the counter for support. Vanessa wanted to see her. This was supposed to be behind them, she thought. Ray told the family Vanessa had pled guilty to shooting him in consideration of a lighter sentence.

"Do you know why Vanessa wants to see me?"

"I'm sorry, ma'am. I was not told anything more than Mrs. Fisher requested to see you."

For several long minutes Miss Jones waited, listening to silence on other end of the call. "You have been approved to see her at the jail when it is convenient for you. The visiting hours are from nine thirty till eleven am and two till four pm

Tuesday, Wednesday, Saturday, and Sunday. Mrs. Fisher will be moved from this facility next Friday." Again she paused, waiting for Cari to speak.

"Miss Jones, I appreciate that you have a job to do, but to be honest I don't intend to honor her request. If Vanessa asks you to contact me again, please tell her I have asked not to be disturbed. Thank you." Shaking, Cari hung up, her head spinning. Why on earth would Vanessa think she would be interested in going to the jail? Hadn't she put everyone through enough pain? Cari decided to talk with Ray. Together they would decide if it would be beneficial to anyone in the family if she talked with Vanessa. Putting all thoughts of the phone call aside, Cari picked up her to-do list and headed down to the shop. She would think about the crazy ex-wife later.

Cଔ Cଔ Cଔ Cଔ Cଔ Cଔ Cଔ Cଔ

Kate could tell something was bothering her mother the moment Cari breezed through the door. Cari reveled in the holiday season and the food baskets were a highlight to her year. Kate would give her mom some space before asking her straight out exactly what was going on.

The weather had finally turned cold and it was a typical November day in New England. The shop was busy with people streaming in, trying to place last-minute orders, enjoying mugs of something warm to drink, and sampling the free cookies Cari laid out.

The door opened and Cari glanced up. "Well, hello there, handsome." Cari greeted Ray with a light peck on the cheek. Seeing his smile warmed her heart and the anxious feeling that had lingered throughout the morning vanished.

He returned the kiss, lightly brushing her lips. "Hello there yourself. Can you spare a few minutes to have lunch with me before the rush starts?"

"How could I resist after you come down here? I may have to take care of customers, too." Cari moved toward the kitchen. "What would you like today?"

A devilish grin slipped over his face and Cari gave him a hard look.

"Something from the menu, Ray," she admonished, suppressing a giggle.

"Surprise me."

"Grab a table and give me a couple of minutes." Cari turned into the kitchen.

Smiling, he noted his girl looked as good walking away as she did walking toward him. He was one lucky guy.

In a few short minutes Cari came to the table carrying a tray with two bowls of steaming chicken vegetable soup, slices of warm crusty bread, sliced fruit, and glasses of iced tea. It smelled wonderful and would certainly fill his grumbling stomach. They made small talk between spoonfuls of soup and mopped up what was left in the bowl with bread crusts.

Satisfied, Ray patted his belly and, with a glint in his eye, said, "I have a surprise for you."

"What do you mean, a surprise? What have you been up to, Ray?"

Extending his hand, he said, "Come out to the truck with me?"

Cari knew Kate needed help. "I can spare a minute." Cari looked over her shoulder and called, "Be right back, Kate. Ray has something to show me."

Cari didn't hear Kate snicker in the kitchen.

"It's a busy day for us. I hope you understand."

"I'm confident you will find this is worth your time." Ray walked to the back of the truck and pulled back the tonneau cover. The bed of the truck was stuffed with bags of potatoes, squash, carrots, cranberry sauce, and a variety of canned food. "I've also managed to get another ten turkeys. Do you think we have enough to fill another ten baskets?" Ray beamed.

Close to tears, Cari croaked, "Where did you get all this food? Do you have any idea how much this means to the families we can help this year?" Digging through the bags and boxes, Cari discovered spices, onions, and other items that would extend well beyond the holidays.

Cari threw her arms around Ray and hugged him tight, forgetting the tenderness in his midsection and caused him to wince slightly. To see the look on her face was worth the minor discomfort he felt.

"Let's get everything inside and we can divide it up." Cari glowed as she grabbed several bags. "We could use an extra pair of hands. Do you want to help? It is the best feeling in the world when you see someone's expression when we deliver the baskets."

"Sweetheart, I thought you'd never ask." Ray grinned and hoisted a few bags up and over the side of the truck. "Let's get cracking, we've got work to do."

Cari shouted for Kate as soon as she got her foot in the door. She trotted out of the kitchen.

"Where did all this come from?" She poked through the bags, checking out the bounty. "This is incredible, Ray!"

"I've been feeling pretty useless for the last couple of weeks. I can't work but I can drive. I know your mom loves to do her baskets and she was telling me how the need was greater than what had been donated. I decided to visit my contractor buddies and see what they could do to help out. I'm proud to say everyone dug deep and donated. This morning I got up and went to the food warehouse, bought everything I could think of, filled the pickup, and here I am." Ray gestured to the bounty on the tables.

While Ray was filling in the details for Kate, Cari called Grace. "Do you have time to come to the shop? No questions. Just get over here. I promise it's a wonderful surprise." Cari put the phone back in its cradle and squeezed Ray again.

"Thank you for all of this. I'm so glad you want to help." Cari's eyes glistened with tears.

"Cari, if it's important to you, then it's important to me. I hope you get used to sharing the load." He leaned in to kiss her softly on the forehead.

"Now, let's get some baskets lined up and start divvying up the loot." Ray gave her a pat on the butt as she went off in search of more baskets.

Kate took another look and did some quick math. "I need more pies and rolls," she said. "Ray, great job today. Don't get too comfy filling baskets, I think I'm going to need some extra hands in the kitchen. You just increased my workload, not that I'm complaining!" Kate made her way to the kitchen, already calling Don on her cell. "Bring anyone who wants to help. We have more baskets to get ready in time for Thanksgiving!"

In a few short hours, the shop was filled with helpers bustling around filling baskets, making pie fillings, and rolling out crusts. Cari was busy keeping the volunteers' coffee cups and plates of cookies full. Content, she looked around her shop overflowing with family and friends working together for a special cause. After all the baskets were stored in the walk-in refrigerator and the last volunteer had left, Cari and Ray asked the family if they wanted to have pizza.

The kids pleaded exhaustion. Kate and Don both said, "Thanks but another time." Jake and Sara promised to reconvene at the shop by nine the next morning. They shut the door tight behind them and hurried to their cars.

Ellie and Shane saw Ray and Cari exchange a private look. Deciding the two lovebirds needed time alone, Ellie piped up, "Mom, Shane and I have Christmas secrets to talk about so we'll grab something and be back bright and early tomorrow to help get the baskets delivered."

After the last round of good-byes Cari turned to Ray. "Thanks for helping out today, Ray. Your contribution is going to make a big difference to a lot of people."

"Alone at last!" Ray pulled Cari into his arms and gave her a hot, deep kiss, causing her toes to curl.

"How does dinner in front of a roaring fire sound, or if you prefer to unwind first, a glass of red wine?" Cari suggested.

Ray didn't have to think about it. "Let's go back to my place and see where the night goes." A sexy smile hovered on his mouth and his fingers lightly caressed her cheek.

Cari gave him a quizzical look but her heart hammered at the implication. "I'll follow you in my car."

"We can have a fireside picnic," Ray suggested.

"That sounds nice," Cari agreed. Her brain was buzzing. Was she ready for the next big leap?

They spread a blanket in front of the fieldstone fireplace that dominated his living room. As the fire blazed, Ray lit candles that cast a romantic glow. Soft piano music emanating from hidden speakers added the final touch of romance.

"This is very romantic. I didn't realize I was dating someone who could create the perfect setting in a few short minutes," Cari murmured. Ray handed her a glass of wine. "I was inspired by the company." Ray's fingers grazed hers, sending her pulse racing. She marveled at the intensity of the sensations that flooded her body every time they touched.

Suddenly shy and unsure, she whispered, "Thank you," and accepted the glass. They had spent many long hours together, just the two of them, but it was understood tonight was going to be different.

"I hope you like this wine, it's a little drier than your usual choice, but I thought it was perfect and it will complement the cheese and fruit. Well, at least that's what Don said when I asked him. It's from his family's winery." Ray chuckled in an attempt to ease the nervous tension in the room.

Cari took a tiny sip. "You can tell Don it was good choice." She closed her eyes, pretending to savor the wine. Instead she took a brief moment to quiet her pounding nerves. Cari felt Ray watching her and opened her eyes.

"Cari," he said huskily, "we don't have to do anything until you're ready. This isn't a race and we have as long as we want or need before we take the next step."

Cari charmed him with an inviting smile. "You need to stop worrying about making me feel comfortable. I don't feel any pressure from you. Relax and drink your wine." Cari filled a plate for each of them and then settled on the blanket next to Ray, their legs touching, and sipped the nerve-soothing wine.

Cari didn't want to break the mood but she needed to bring up a difficult subject before things went any further. Cari took Ray's hand. "I got a very strange call today from Vanessa's lawyer's office. I've been trying to find a way to bring it up but I haven't any idea how to do that except by being direct and to the point."

Ray gave her his full attention. "And what exactly did they want, and why didn't they call me? I'm not happy to hear that Vanessa is attempting to contact you, even if it is through her lawyer. I don't want my ex-wife anywhere near our families, or you for that matter! I'm going to the jail tomorrow to find out what the hell she is up to now!"

Holding tight, Cari got his attention. "Ray, I was perplexed when Miss Jones called. Heck, I still am. Apparently, Vanessa has requested to see me before she's moved from the county jail. Supposedly, she has to talk to me. I have to admit I'm curious. Do you think I should go?"

"NO! You shouldn't get within a hundred yards of the jail, let alone actually sit and talk with Vanessa!"

"I don't want to go but there's a part of me that feels compelled to find out what she wants from me. If I decide to go it will be my decision. If she gets nasty I can leave," Cari reassured him.

Ray became unusually quiet, spinning scenarios in his mind. What could Vanessa gain from talking to Cari? The only positive was Vanessa couldn't harm her.

Cari released his hand and moved to stand in front of the fire, poking it and adding another log to the blaze. She had had all day to mull over the request. She needed to give Ray the same courtesy. Staring at the fire and lost in thought, Cari didn't hear Ray come up behind her. He pulled Cari into his arms, holding her close.

"If you are determined to see her, I'll take you. She's never going to be able to hurt either of us again. Maybe she wants to apologize, although I have no idea how anyone could apologize for something like this. You tell me when and then it will be behind us." Ray nuzzled her neck, distracting her with feather-like kisses on the back of her neck.

It was difficult to concentrate on words as he was doing his best to change the current topic.

"Sunday. Then we can concentrate on the future." Cari turned to meet his mouth with hers, matching the heat of his searing kiss.

They eased onto the blanket, basking in the heat of the fire. Ray covered her face and eyes with tender kisses and when he claimed her lips he devoured them with an intensity and passion that caught her by surprise. His hands traveled slowly down her arms, lightly caressing the soft underside, and ended at her fingertips. His lips brushed her upturned palms and worked his way back to her mouth, leaving a trail of kisses that made her weak with desire.

Cari couldn't remember feeling this alive. The fire inside of her burned uncontrollably. Ray was slowly driving her out of her mind as he exploring every inch of her curves. She longed to rip their clothes off and expose sweat-slicked skin.

Cautiously at first, Cari allowed her hands to slide down his soft plaid shirt. She pulled it free, exposing soft and warm flesh. Her hand lightly caressed his long muscular back, coming to rest on his belt. Shyness overcame her but her need for him was stronger.

Ray felt her hesitation. He gently reached out from under her, waiting for a signal she was ready for more. Cari took his hand and helped him slowly unbutton her top. Her skin was quivering in anticipation.

Following her lead, Ray peeled off what was left of his clothes. Cari watched them fall to the floor. Ray lowered himself to the floor, once again facing the woman he loved. They didn't speak with words. Discovering the wonder of the other's touch, their need and desire were all that mattered, their bodies riding and falling like a boat on the ocean.

They came together, two bodies, hearts, and souls in one glorious, perfect union.

Drained and covered with a fine mist of sweat and pleasure, Ray pulled a blanket over them. Cari sighed softly.

Ray cradled her in his arms. "Sweetheart?" he spoke softly.

In the dim firelight Ray couldn't see the Cheshire cat grin she wore.

Breathless, she said, "Ray, this has been the most amazingly wonderful, truly perfect romantic moment I've ever had!" In the space of one evening she had gone from a woman in love with a man, not sure where it would lead, to a woman who was loved in return and looking forward to what would come next.

As if reading her thoughts, Ray kissed her softly. "Our adventure will continue."

Cari snuggled deep in the circle of his love, pleased at how her life had changed. In spite of herself, she shivered, but she didn't want to move or break the spell woven around them. Ray kissed her hair. He got up to put another log on the fire and grabbed a blanket from the sofa. They curled up together, watching the flames until they were ready to do the dance of love again.

Chapter Eighteen

THIS YEAR CARI HAD SO MANY THINGS TO BE THANKFUL FOR, an amazing man that made her heart sing, children who were happy and healthy, wonderful friends, and a thriving business that enabled her to give back to others. Surprisingly, after a night with very little sleep, she felt like she could conquer the world. When she lightly kissed Ray good-bye, he hadn't stirred. He was exhausted. She got his coffee ready and left a note reminding him they were going to start delivering the baskets early afternoon.

She arrived at the shop early and enjoyed the peace before chaos would erupt. The shop would be packed with customers picking up items for their holiday meals and dropping off last-minute additions to the food baskets. Generosity seemed to be contagious.

Her kids, along with Jake and Sara, were hanging out in the kitchen enjoying a cup of coffee after cleaning the kitchen. Cari watched them, unobserved, for a few minutes. They looked like a family. "Hey, kids!" she called out. "Who wants to get the Christmas decorations from storage? I'd like to decorate the shop before we close today. It's going to be hectic here on Friday and it's important to create a festive holiday atmosphere for our customers. Historically it spurs them into buying and placing lots of orders." She laughed.

Everyone jumped up, ready to help. The guys went to retrieve the boxes while the girls walked out front, interested to see what Cari had in mind. Kate was in charge of lights and she showed Sara and Ellie how to drape them around the windows. Shane and Jake rearranged the tables and chairs to make room for the tree that Don was putting in the stand.

Ray stood on the sidewalk watching the buzz of activity inside. As usual, Cari had everything under control, directing the decorating, gesturing where lights should be strung and the tree to be placed. If he had any doubts about this woman, seeing her in action with his kids made it disappear.

Over the din Cari didn't hear the door open. Ray crept up, twirled her around, and smothered her with an ardent kiss. The group discreetly looked away but poked each other to make sure no one missed this very public display of affection.

"Next time you think about sneaking out of the house, think again. Please take a couple of minutes to wake me up. I need a proper kiss good-bye," Ray teased in a whisper for her ears alone.

Sara was closest to the pair and could just make out what Ray was saying. She caught the group's attention and bobbed her head in their direction. It was really happening; Ray and Cari were falling in love.

Kate wore a smug little smile. Part of her plan was working out. But she wasn't going to rest until Ray and her mother tied the knot.

Ray reluctantly released Cari. In an attempt to calm her racing heart, she ran a hand over her hair. Casually she turned, surveying the room. Thankfully, no one seemed to have noticed as everyone was busy finishing the decorations. Glancing at her watch, she saw it was time to start the deliveries.

Cari savored every moment with her family and dear friends. The holidays hadn't been this much fun since before Ben had died. "Does anyone want to come for potluck tonight?"

"Count us in, Mom. We'd planned on coming for dinner even if you hadn't asked," Shane said with a grin. "Actually, we were going to finish up the painting in the sunroom and Ray has the built-ins done so we're going to install them, right?" Shane had turned to address Ray.

Ray nodded. "Yes, the cabinets are done. I think we can move the furniture back in the room. You should be able to decorate for Christmas soon, love. I'm sorry I wasn't able to get it done for Thanksgiving. It would have been nice to have it ready for tomorrow."

Forgetting they had an audience, Cari flung her arms around his neck. "I can't wait to see it all done!" she beamed. "Let's get things wrapped up here. I have a to-do list a mile long and I would like to get home at some point before dark. We'll have a quick dinner—hamburgers and hot dogs—and hopefully everyone will be ready for a traditional meal tomorrow."

Everyone agreed to meet at Cari's when they were finished delivering their baskets.

ᬀ ᬀ ᬀ ᬀ ᬀ ᬀ ᬀ ᬀ

Ray and Cari were at the last family on their list. It was a young couple with a newborn and two more little ones under five. In addition to the fixings for a Thanksgiving feast, they had bags of formula, diapers, and other nonperishable food. The father had been out of work for months, and they were living from one unemployment check to another. Cari wondered if Jake needed someone to drive a snowplow for the coming winter.

Ray drove Cari home. Exhausted, Cari put her head back and closed her eyes. Ray held her hand, keeping one eye on her and the other on the road. He was constantly amazed by her selflessness. Tough times had knocked on her door a time or two, but it didn't stop her. Instead, it had inspired her to help others.

Ray came to a stop and Cari sat up, blinking away the fog that settled over her. "Oh good, someone brought my car." She glanced around the driveway, noticing her and Ray's kids were accounted for. She hopped out of the truck and they walked hand in hand to the house.

Before they reached the door Cari stopped and turned to Ray.

"Thank you for today. It meant a great deal to me that you were with me."

"I must admit, you would never have been able to describe how it would make me feel, to give a basket to someone in need of a helping hand. I should be thanking you. I've never had a day like today." Ray was humbled by what he had witnessed. He never knew so many families in and around Loudon needed help.

Cari laid her hand softly on Ray's cheek. "I've never asked anyone to go with me. I'm glad I got to share this with you."

The door burst open and Shane jogged past them on the way to his truck. "Hey, you two, are you coming in?"

The kitchen was filled with mouthwatering aromas. The girls peeled, chopped, and mixed, and Ellie had just finished setting the table and moved on to create a masterpiece for the centerpiece. Cari longed to sit for a couple of minutes and savor a few minutes of silence, but there would be time for that tomorrow night.

"Coffee or something stronger? It's crazy in here. . . ." Cari turned to Ray as they walked into the hub of activity.

As if reading her mind, Ray pointed to a chair. "Sure, but how about I wait on you for a change. Go, sit, put your feet up, and relax for five minutes. I'm going to go see what our boys are up to." Ray dropped a kiss on her hair before going down the hall.

Cari loved her home bursting with people enjoying themselves. She heard shouting from the front of the house and pulled herself up from the chair just as Grace and Charlie popped in, loaded down with bags of Chinese takeout. Charlie held up chopsticks. "There's nothing like starting a traditional New England holiday with Chinese. It's the only meal I know that will guarantee you'll be ready for your next meal."

Laughing at her husband, Grace waved at Cari. "I've got this. I know where the plates are and I'll put everything on the counter, buffet style."

Cari marveled at her friend. Grace was one of a kind. Takeout, instead of cooking—that made things easy! "GF, thanks," was all Cari could muster.

Ray pulled back a drop cloth that covered the doorway to the sunroom. He stopped midstep, a lump lodged in his throat. The boys - Jake, Don, and Shane had just finished installing the cabinet he'd built. Jake wiped the dust off the top as Don was testing the hinges, confirming they worked smoothly. The wood stove sat prepped with kindling, waiting for a match strike to bring the wood to life. Sara walked up from behind and tapped him on the shoulder. Pressed curtains lay folded in her arms, ready to be hung on rods. He moved aside to let her pass. Jake hurried over to lend his wife a hand. Finally, he cleared his throat. "Uh, gentlemen, Sara, what's going on in here?"

Shane and Don turned around, amused to see Ray stumbling over his words.

"Ray, what are you doing in here? This is supposed to be a surprise for Mom. You should go and keep her occupied so she doesn't wander in here, too." Shane tried to be stern but was having trouble hiding his excitement.

"Carry on," was all Ray could utter.

He backed away from the drop cloth and slumped down on the stairs. He was very proud of these boys. They had given up their personal time to help him out and do something special for Cari. He was grateful beyond words. Composed, he ambled back to the kitchen. With all the activity in the house, Ray didn't think Cari would suspect anything was amiss, until it was time for the grand unveiling.

Over the next half hour or so, the kids drifted in to dinner. Shane gave Ray a slight nod, indicating everything was ready. After the dishes were cleared and everyone was relaxing, Shane glanced at his partners in crime.

"Hey, Mom. We've finished painting. Do you want to see how the color looks? I think the walls turned out pretty good." Shane knew his mother wouldn't be able to resist.

"I'd love to. Ray, do you want to come?" Cari held out her hand to him. Ray let her pull him down the hall.

"Let's see how these boys slap on paint." Looking over Cari's head, he mouthed a "thank you."

Leading the way down the hall, Shane pulled back the drop cloth, and ushered his Mom through the doorway.

"Oh my stars!" Cari cried as she entered the fully furnished room. The wood stove crackled with a fire. Cari crossed the room to her prized possession, the piano. Casually she ran her hand across the keys, visually circling the room to absorb every detail. "Who hung the curtains? They are perfect, billowy white clouds floating against the soft blue sky on a summer day." Then she saw the cabinets Ray built. Turning to him, she mused, "When did you have time to finish and install it?"

"I didn't, our sons got together and took it upon themselves to finish it." He turned to the group. "I have to say, I'm very proud of all of you."

Cari sank into the overstuffed loveseat and patted the empty space, indicating Ray to join her. He dropped beside her, slipping his arm around her shoulders and pulling her close.

"Everyone sit, let's enjoy the fire and the evening." It was a perfect beginning for the holiday season.

03 03 03 03 03 03 03 03

Cari woke to muffled sounds coming from her kitchen. The rich aroma of coffee wafted to her bedroom. Sliding her feet into fleece-lined slippers and tightly tying a warm fuzzy bathrobe, she stumbled to the kitchen. She discovered Ellie was setting out a light breakfast for the two of them.

"Good morning, sleepyhead," Ellie chirped.

"How long have you been up?" Cari stifled a yawn.

"Well, let's see, long enough to have finished stuffing the bird and put it in the oven. And of course I made coffee!"

Cari poured two mugs and placed them on the breakfast bar. She picked up the plate of fruit and muffins that were on the counter. "This is a nice treat, Pixie." Smiling at her youngest daughter, "There are times I have to remind myself you're not a little girl anymore. You've really grown up this last year."

Cari glanced at the clock. "What time did Kate say she'd be over?"

"I'm not sure. Maybe in a couple of hours." Ellie paused in midthought. "Um, Mom, can I talk to you before everything gets crazy around here?"

"Ellie, of course you can. You don't have to ask. Is everything going well at school?"

"School's great, no worries there. I want to talk to you about Ray." Waiting until she had her mother's full attention, Ellie continued.

"This is a little embarrassing but it's like this." Ellie took a deep breath. "I really like Ray, and if you decide that you want him to spend the night or something, it's okay with me. I'll admit at first I wasn't sure how I'd feel. I like the idea of you dating but it was going to be weird having some strange guy hanging around. But now that you're dating Ray, I'm really fine with, well, you know, everything that comes with it."

Cari slowly exhaled, unaware she had been holding her breath. "I appreciate how hard this must be for you, I care for Ray a great deal, and we have fun together. There might come a time when we decide to take our relationship to the next level but for now I'm happy where everything stands. He's an amazing man and hopefully he'll be around for a long, long time." Cari leaned in and hugged Ellie. "We should enjoy our breakfast before our company arrives and they find us sitting here in our pj's."

The day flew by with last-minute preparations and the hustle and bustle that goes with a holiday. Everyone arrived in plenty of time to help and at long last gathered around the dining room table, which was laden with every edible creation desired. At the head of the table was Cari with Ray to her right. Shane was directly across from his mother, flanked by his sisters on either side of him. The rest of the group filled in around the table.

Ray clinked his glass with a spoon. "May I please have everyone's attention for just a moment? If no one has any objection, before we stuff ourselves, I would like to offer a toast." Not wanting to step on toes, he paused and looked at Shane. With a slight nod, Shane gave him the floor.

Ray pushed his chair back and rose to hold up his beer glass. "As you know I'm a man of few words. I would like to thank Cari and her family for inviting Jake, Sara, and me to share this holiday with them. I have many things to be thankful for this year." Looking at Jake and Sara, he continued, "To Jake and Sara, who are the best son and daughter a man could ask for. Without you, I would be lost. To the McKenna clan, you've welcomed us into your home and hearts as a part of your family. You are an incredible group—your mother can be proud of each one of you. Grace and Charlie, you've included me as a part of your extended family, you humble me. Lastly, Cari, because of your crazy fearlessness I'm standing here today. If you hadn't come around my garage brandishing a rake I shudder to think what might have happened. You are my angel." He raised his glass a little higher. "To Cari." Everyone at the table joined him in unison, "To Cari."

Cari's eyes welled up with tears, not knowing what to say or do to redirect everyone's attention. Thankfully, Jake noticed and jumped in.

Jake cleared his throat, and grasped Sara's hand in his. "Sara and I have something we want to share with everyone here. Dad? You're going to be a grandpa." Jake and Sara glowed.

Everyone began talking at once, offering congratulations to the new parents.

Shane waited until everyone quieted down before speaking. "My sisters and I are thankful for our mom. She is an amazing person and the example she has always set helped us become the people we are today. But this year, in addition to toasting Mom, we would like to include Ray."

Shane paused to look at the people assembled around the table. "Ray, we'd like to thank you for putting a sparkle into our mother's eyes." Before Cari started to cry, Shane finished up. "To everyone gathered around this table, thank you for making our family complete." They raised their glasses and said, "To family!"

Grace looked at Charlie and nudged him to stand. "On behalf of Grace and me, thank you for sharing this day with us, to another year of being with the people we love the most."

Cari stood up. "Well, I guess it's up to me to wrap this up before the food gets cold. I'm thankful for many things. But the most important things are right here, in this house, the people I have the privilege to share my life with. I love you all. Happy Thanksgiving."

Cari sat down, taking Ray's and Grace's hands in hers. Nine pairs of eyes rested on her. "It has been quite a year. A tree dropped on my house. I have the best friends a girl could ask for, amazing children, all six of you." Her gaze slid over her children and Don to Jake and Sara. "And I discovered that an old friendship is the perfect starting point for a new romance."

Ray squeezed her hand in agreement. "I couldn't ask for anything more. I am truly blessed." Cari released Grace's hand and picked up her water glass. "To the first of many holidays in this old house, filled to the rafters with those we love, and the next generation yet to come.

"Here, here!" Everyone chimed in.

"So who's going to pass the potatoes?" Cari laughed.

Chapter Nineteen

CARI HAD A BAD CASE OF NERVOUS ENERGY. Ray would be picking her up in a few minutes to drive her to the jail. It was visiting day with Vanessa. She still wasn't sure she was doing the right thing. A horn honked, interrupting her thoughts. Peeking out the window, she saw Ray was right on time. Couldn't he ever be a little late? she wondered.

Cari opened the door, hurried down the walkway, and jumped into the warm truck before Ray had a chance to get out and open the door. She leaned over to peck his lips. "Let's go. I want to get this over with as soon as possible."

"Sweetheart, we don't have to go. We can forget about it and do something else today." Ray didn't attempt to put the truck in gear. He was hoping Cari would have changed her mind by this morning.

Cari smiled at the term of endearment. Shaking her head, she said firmly, "Nope, we're going. I'm going to listen to what Vanessa has to say and when we leave the jail, we're not looking back."

"Alright, you're the boss." Ray backed the truck out of the driveway. They stopped for coffee and drove the remainder of the trip in silence. Ray eased into a parking spot in the visitors' lot. He shut off the car and they both sat, sipping their now lukewarm coffee, neither of them in a hurry to get out. "Do you want me in the room with you or to wait outside?"

Cari looked directly at him and without hesitation said, "I don't want you anywhere near her. I can handle this." Cari knew she was being irrational. Vanessa wouldn't be able to physically harm either of them. She had no intention of letting Vanessa know Ray was with her.

Ray reluctantly agreed. "I will be just outside the room, if at any point you need me!"

Cari sat at the visitors' table impatiently waiting for Vanessa. "These chairs are very uncomfortable," she said out loud. Even though there wasn't anyone that could hear her, it helped to have noise in the barren room. She looked around, curious. "This room is depressing. I wonder if this is what the entire building is like."

Metal grated on metal as a heavy door slowly slid open. Vanessa was escorted into the room, handcuffed, by a female guard who steered her to a metal chair on the opposite side of the table. Vanessa looked tiny and frail in the bright orange jumpsuit with her dull blond hair pulled into a severe ponytail and face devoid of makeup.

"Cari, thank you for coming. I didn't think you would." Vanessa's voice was barely audible.

Cari leaned forward to hear her. "Vanessa, I don't have any idea why you would want to see me. We've never been friends." Cari paused, letting her words hang in the air.

"I'm sure you were surprised to get the call from my lawyer's office. Since I've been here, they put me on medication and it has helped quiet the crazy voices in my head. I had to tell you I'm sorry about what happened that day at Ray's. I never meant to shoot him. I still have a hard time believing I had a gun." Vanessa's words were stilted.

Vanessa waited, hoping Cari would say something. The silence went on for several minutes. "I assume you've been told I'm going away, for quite a long time, and there is still the issue of what I did to Stan. California hasn't handed down its verdict yet. But out of everything I've done it's nothing compared to what I have done to my son. For many years, I didn't want to be a mother. I thought if people saw that I had a grown son they'd think I was old."

Vanessa could see Cari was stunned. Vanessa held up her hand, "Please, indulge me another minute. I would like to ask you to do something, not for me, but for Jake and

Sara. Will you be there for them, like a mother should be? I understand Sara's family lives in the Midwest. I'm sure there are times that she feels lost without her mom around, and Jake, well, he never had a real mother. You know when I lived here I used to watch you with your kids. I was jealous of how easy it was for you. You were a great mom and I'm sure that hasn't changed. It would be good for Jake to have a mother figure he could lean on from time to time. You know, for the things he can't talk to Ray about."

Cari sat glued to the chair. Her heart broke for Jake. Vanessa was shoving him out of her life permanently and he didn't even have a choice in the matter.

"Vanessa, after some time has passed you could reach out to Jake and work on your relationship. A son's love for his mother is unconditional, no matter what has happened between them."

"No," Vanessa said vehemently. "Jake is done with me forever. He will never be able to forgive what I did to his father. I've come to terms with that. I beg you, please think about my request, for my son and his family." Vanessa turned to the guard. "I'm ready to go back. Please."

Before Cari could articulate a single coherent thought, Vanessa was gone. Cari had things she wanted to say to her but didn't get the opportunity. She pulled herself together, stood up, and left the small barren room. Ray was waiting for Cari as she exited the room.

"Take me home."

Ray slipped his arm around Cari and they walked out of the jail into the weak sunshine. He would be patient, confident she would tell him what happened behind the locked door.

They spent the rest of the morning puttering in Ray's wood shop, working on her long overdue shelf project. Gifford slept in a bed tucked into the corner. Ray kept a watchful eye on Cari as she cautiously used the table saw. Methodically, she cut the boards to length and switched to the scroll saw to cut out decorative support brackets. Once the shelf was assembled, she sanded it with slow deliberate motions, careful to create a smooth surface. Cari finished up with a thin coat of stain and left it to dry, satisfied with her first piece of furniture.

Late in the afternoon, they strolled through the back-yard to Cari's. Putting the last of the turkey leftovers in a soup pot to simmer on the wood stove, they plopped on the sofa, feet propped up and toes wiggling in the warmth of the fire.

Cari had avoided the topic of Vanessa long enough. "Ray, about today," she began. "The conversation with Vanessa was surreal. Basically, she asked me to look after Jake as a mother and be there for Sara. She apologized for shooting you but her main focus was Jake and her failure as a mother. I tried to suggest she reach out to him but she told me the relationship was over and to step in. Honestly, I think she was being sincere, but I still can't figure it out. She's on meds and acting normal, why wouldn't she want to try with Jake? Eventually he could forgive her and they could e-mail or, heck, I don't know what they could have. This visit broke my heart. You're going to hate to hear this, but I feel sorry for Vanessa."

"That is so typical of Vanessa. Hurt people and run, don't stand up and admit to a mistake, but let someone else clean up the mess. I'm disappointed that she wouldn't try to reach out to Jake and fix things, too. She's going away for a long time."

Frustrated, Ray ran his fingers over his beard. "Vanessa isn't the woman I married. She was tough as nails, but it sounds like whatever this breakdown was left her a shell of who she used to be. When he's ready, Jake will have to decide if he wants to salvage his relationship with his mother. And it goes without saying, but I'll support whatever he decides to do."

"At least we know that she is taking medication and she doesn't seem delusional anymore. She was sad but matter-of-fact about everything. I guess for Vanessa, going to jail was a blessing in disguise. She got the help she desperately needed. The unfortunate thing is so many people got hurt during her downward spiral."

Nuzzling behind her ear, Ray whispered, "Cari, I love that you are a wonderful, compassionate woman and remember, something wonderful came out of this mess—us!"

Cari giggled. "Should I send Vanessa a note to thank her for opening my eyes?"

"Nah, she's on a need-to-know basis only." Ray tickled her ribs and Cari let out a loud squeal of protest.

"If the soup burns, you're cleaning the pot, sir." Moments later, everything was forgotten as they became lost in each other's arms.

Chapter Twenty

THE WEEKS LEADING UP TO THE CHRISTMAS HOLIDAYS WERE A FLURRY OF ACTIVITY. What's Perkin' had been extremely busy and Ellie came to help out once the semester was over. Cari's parents, Dave and Susan Riley, came to town for the holidays and, without being asked, jumped in to help out at the shop. Cari was exceedingly grateful for the extra hands. It was just like her first few years in business with her mom and dad helping out, preparing and delivering baked items during the holiday rush.

Ray had been cleared to go back to work and was finishing a kitchen project. Everyone was coming to the McKenna home for Christmas Eve. The plan was to spend the night, wake up to gifts under the tree and a big breakfast, have a fabulous supper, and spend the rest of the day together.

As the holiday grew closer, Cari was fretting. She was one present short. The perfect gift for Ray escaped her. Long hours had been spent contemplating many ideas but so far, nothing struck her.

The couple spent all their free time together but had yet to spend an entire night under the same roof. Heck, they hadn't even said those three little words yet. They used various terms of endearment—"sweetheart" primarily—but Cari already knew that she had given her heart to Ray.

Sara had confided to Kate that she was feeling down. Her mother, Vera, called to break the news that they weren't going to make the drive for Christmas; she had broken her ankle after slipping on an ice-covered sidewalk. Kate shared the information with Cari, who made it a point to involve Sara with their traditional family activities.

Sara was at the counter, busy decorating Christmas cookies. The shop couldn't keep them in stock. Cari set a cup of herbal tea, sweetened with a dribble of honey, in front of her.

"They're beautiful, Sara. You have a real knack for cookie decorating." Cari reached out to tuck a stray lock of hair behind her ear. "How are you feeling today? You look a touch pale, have you had something to eat? You've been at this for quite a while now." Cari said gently.

Sara's pregnancy was draining her energy. She decided to appoint an office manager for her real estate business and take time off from the daily grind, checking in every few days.

"I've nibbled on a couple of cookies and I'm feeling so much better, more like myself." Sara turned to give a side view, pulling her apron tight to show off an obvious baby bump. Clearly excited, she said, "Look, I'm starting to show already!"

Cari admired her expanding waistline. "You've really popped out there, haven't you? Before long we'll need to go shopping for new clothes," Cari joked.

"I know, won't that be fun? Maybe all of us girls can make a day of it, go out to lunch, get pedicures, and shop." Sara's voice dropped to just above a whisper.

"Cari, can you keep a secret?"

Cari slowly nodded her head.

"I haven't said anything to Jake yet, but the doctor thinks we might be having twins. I have to go for an ultrasound after the holidays."

Cari squealed in delight and grabbed Sara's hands, twirling her around. "When you know, make sure to fill me in. We'll make sure you get two of everything at your shower."

CB CB CB CB CB CB CB CB

Alone in the kitchen, Cari groaned inwardly as she flipped through a sales flyer. Only two days left to find Ray's gift. She needed inspiration and she needed it to strike soon. Cari turned off most of the lights and gave the counter one last swipe with the cleaning cloth. She glanced at the clock over the door, reluctant to go home. Ray would be working late tonight. It's funny how she never used to give it a thought, going home to an empty house. How quickly things change. Now, when she pulled up their street and saw his truck, she could feel a smile spread across her face, she couldn't wait see him.

An idea started to gel: a space in her house devoted to Ray. She yanked off her apron and pulled the door firmly shut behind her. She hoped the furniture store was still open and that they would deliver by Christmas Eve.

Cari made short work of the large furniture store, sitting in overstuffed chairs with ottomans and comfy recliners. Whatever she chose it would have to coordinate with the furniture in her sunroom while also being comfortable for her man. She was going to give Ray her heart for Christmas and ask him to move in with her. Hopefully he wouldn't feel she was rushing him into a commitment. They spent all their free time together and Cari decided it was the next logical step.

Cari could see the sales clerk watching as she moved around the showroom acting like Goldilocks, until finally she sunk into a deep green oversize chair with a matching ottoman. Cari closed her eyes, envisioning the two of them cuddled up, watching a movie on a frosty winter night.

"I'll take the set." Cari patted the plush arm cushion and smiled to the clerk.

"Excellent choice, I can have it delivered in eight weeks." The clerk pulled out the sales book to write up the sale.

"This is a Christmas present. I need to have it delivered tomorrow."

"I'm sorry, ma'am, but we don't carry this particular set as a stock item. I couldn't possibly get it delivered in time for the holiday. In addition, our delivery teams are extremely busy with other orders." Irritated, the clerk was thinking about her lost commission.

"I'll buy the floor model and my son will pick it up. Problem solved!"

"Ma'am, we don't sell the floor models."

Exasperated, Cari gestured around the store. "I see floor models with price tags stating they're available for immediate delivery. I'd like to speak with the store manager, please." Now that she found the perfect gift, she wasn't leaving without purchasing it. The clerk stalked off in search of the manager.

Cari settled in the chair and propped her feet up to wait. Cari couldn't wait for Ray to "open" his present and she could broach the "let's live together" conversation. Digging in her handbag, she pulled her cell phone out and dialed.

"Hi, Shane. I have a favor to ask. Would you be able to run to Smithfield tomorrow, to Simon's Furniture Store out on Highway 20? I found the perfect gift for Ray—a chair and ottoman—but the store can't deliver. You'll need Don to carry it in the house.

"Not a problem, Mom. We'll get it tomorrow and drop it off. Where do you want us to put it?" Shane was surprised she wanted them to take it to her house when they'd just have to move it to Ray's after the holiday.

"Put it in the back corner of the sunroom and drape a Christmas blanket over it. I'll see if I can camouflage it. Oh, we'll put the ottoman in my room, one less thing for Ray to accidently see. I want it to be a surprise."

Shane smiled into the phone. "Don't worry, Mom. Don and I have it covered."

Chapter Twenty-One

"**M**erry Christmas Eve!" Cari happily greeted each customer as they came in to pick up last-minute goodies to either give as a gift or enjoy themselves. People were clearing the shelves of all the baked goods and the register hummed. Main Street was buzzing with last-minute shoppers full of the Christmas spirit. Cari couldn't remember a better holiday season for the store.

Cari walked outside to gaze up at the clear blue sky. Not a single flake of snow predicted in the weather forecast. Cari sighed. She believed snow was Mother Nature's gift that she gave for Christmas each year. However, this year it looked like Mother Nature was giving a green Christmas. Cari greeted friends and neighbors as they rushed past her on the sidewalk, in a hurry to finish last-minute errands before heading home to spend time with their families.

Cari watched Ray as he parked across the street. Waving, he jogged over. Gathering her in his arms, he warmed her lips with a kiss.

"Hey, beautiful!" he said. "What time are you closing up and going home?" Ray pushed the door open and held it for her as she walked in ahead of him. He marveled at the changes that had taken place over the last couple of months. What's Perkin' had always been his favorite place but after one pointed conversation with Cari, he stopped acting like a customer and got the message to help himself. In the beginning, Ray wasn't sure if it would bother Kate. Without blinking an eye, Kate accepted him digging in the refrigerator or grabbing a plate of the daily special. In return, he helped out whenever an extra set of hands were needed for cleaning, fixing something, or hauling boxes.

"You haven't said what time you're going to close down." Ray prodded her for an answer.

"Soon. There are a few more orders that need to be picked up. I already sent Kate and Ellie home. Sara was in earlier. I shooed her out the door, making her promise she would go home and rest. We're going to have a couple of busy days and I don't want her getting overtired."

A look of concern crossed Ray's face. "Do you think there is a reason to be concerned?"

"No, it's normal in the early stages of a pregnancy for the mother to be tired. In her second trimester, she'll have energy to burn, and during the third we can expect exhaustion to set in." Cari did her best to reassure him. "Remember, I've done this couple of times. She'll be fine."

Glancing at her watch, confident that the coast must be clear at her place, she said, "Why don't you go home and relax? I'll call when I've made myself presentable. Maybe we can have a quiet drink before things get really busy?"

"That sounds like a terrific idea. I'll call you later." Ray was anxious to get going. He had one last stop to make on the way home and he still had to wrap a few things for the kids. Ray was halfway out the door when he turned around, swept her off the stool, and covered her mouth with a slow and silky kiss. "See you soon, love." For the first time in years, he was full of the Christmas spirit. Cari saved his life, in more ways than one.

As fast as he had embraced her, she was released. Without looking back, he strode out the door.

Amused, Cari watched him strut to his truck. Instead of getting in he continued down the street. "Hmm, everyone is entitled to a few secrets this time of year," she said to herself.

The last customer came and Cari sent them off with an extra dozen cookies. She finished straightening the tables and chairs and turned off the overhead lights, taking a moment to savor the glow of the holiday lights. Gazing out the front window, she hugged her arms around herself and prayed that when she came back to her shop her life was going to go in a new direction. She searched the sky for a snowflake or two, but there was none to be had. It was time to join her family.

CB CB CB CB CB CB CB CB

The festivities were in full swing when Ray arrived. A buffet was set up in the dining room and Cari's dad, Dave, had arranged a temporary bar on the sideboard. Christmas music drifted through speakers, adding to the festive ambiance.

Ray's gaze swept the room. Not finding Cari, he ducked into the kitchen. She was pulling a large foil-wrapped platter from the oven. He tiptoed up to her, patiently waiting for her to set the platter down. Before she removed the pot-holders from her hands, he slipped his arms around her waist and whispered in her ear, "Merry Christmas, sweetheart." Ray's voice was like honey in her ear.

Cari leaned back into him, soaking up the warmth of his arms and feeling happy he had finally arrived. Like a small child bursting with a secret, she asked, "I got Gifford a present. Do you want it now or later? And I got you a little something, too."

"Oh, I like how that sounds!" he teased. "If it's alright with you, let's wait until later. Remember, you have guests."

Cari blushed and smoothed her dress down. "That is not what I was referring to and you know it," she chided with a grin. Offering her hand, she said, "Let's join everyone and eat."

After a good dent was made in the food and drinks, everyone lounged in the sunroom.

"The tree is stunning this year!" Ellie said to the group. "I'm glad you got a huge tree, it filled up the space nicely."

Cari's gaze went to the top and rested on the angel. "I think it's the best tree we've had in a long time," she murmured. Rising, she adjusted a couple of ornaments and glanced out the French doors, silently praying for a white Christmas.

"Oh, look it's started to snow!" she exclaimed with wonder.

Ray joined her and, to his amazement, she threw open the door to let the cool air wash over them.

"I just love the first snowfall each year. It's magical!" Cari slipped her arm around Ray's waist and tugged him out into the falling snow.

Cari didn't notice that Ray pulled the door shut behind them.

"Hmmm, life doesn't get much better than this, you know. A white Christmas, our families inside, and your arms wrapped around me. It's the perfect night. Mother Nature delivered our gift just in time."

Ray chuckled and gazed into her eyes. "You asked for snow? If I had known that I wouldn't have driven myself crazy trying to decide what I should give you."

Ray and Cari watched lazy snowflakes make their way to the grass, changing from a green to white blanket as it started to accumulate.

Cari shivered with cold. "We should go inside before we catch a cold."

"Wait, for just a minute." Ray turned to Cari so he could look into her eyes. "Many years ago my dad told me to fall in love with my best friend. It took a lot of years but finally I understand what he was trying to tell me. I listened to his sage advice. Cari we have fun together, we laugh together, and we love together. You're the last person I want to see before I fall asleep and the first person I want to kiss each morning. So, Cari, before we freeze to death, I have one question to ask you." Ray reached into his pocket and dropped to one knee.

"Marry me?" Ray popped open a small black velvet box. Nestled inside was the most beautiful ring she had ever seen, a single solitaire diamond resting on black velvet.

Tears of joy streamed down her face. "Are you sure?" The sound of Cari's laughter drifted to the family inside. They rushed to the doors to see what was going on.

Ellie grabbed Kate's arm. "Look, Ray's on one knee!" Kate, Ellie, and Sara squealed with excitement.

"Do you think she said yes?" Ellie demanded.

"If she didn't, we'll say yes for her." Kate was laughing and crying at the same time.

Ray didn't expect the tears and laughter.

Cari pulled him up off the snow-covered deck and covered his face with kisses. "YES, I'll marry you," she said and gave Ray her left hand to slide the ring on her finger. "Come with me. I have a question for you, too."

She grabbed his hand, flung open the doors, and hurried past the group eavesdropping near the door. For the first time, Ray noticed a holiday blanket thrown in a heap in the shadows.

"Ray, I love you more than you'll ever know. I was going to give you this for Christmas and ask you to live with me." Cari whisked the blanket off, exposing the chair and ottoman, as well as a dog bed for Gifford.

With a lump firmly lodged in his throat, Ray picked her up and twirled her around the room.

"Sweetheart, I'm happy to live with you all the rest of our days!"

Epilogue

SINCE THE SNOW BEGAN ON CHRISTMAS EVE, it continued for the next seven days. The sun finally made an appearance on New Year's Day. Cari peeked out the windows. Light bounced off the snow in the backyard like jewels peeking out from under a white blanket. The boys shoveled a path from the back deck to the garden, ending at the newly planted tree. Baskets of pine boughs tied with dark purple ribbons stood next to empty plant stands waiting for the white poinsettias that would adorn them.

It had been unanimous. The family was thrilled to combine the Davises and the McKennas into one large family. Kate and Ellie were delighted to have Ray officially become their stepfather. They were thrilled to have a new baby on the way so they could become aunties.

Cari heard the hum of voices downstairs. The girls would be up shortly. Cari finished her makeup and was almost ready to step into her dress. It had been a hectic week since she accepted Ray's proposal. Susan had joked they should start their new life on the first day of the new year. Cari and Ray decided it was a great way to start off so preparations went into high gear to pull together a wedding. The weather was finally cooperating.

"Mom, are you ready?" Kate asked as she knocked and tentatively pushed the door open.

Cari was standing in front of the mirror, looking at her daughters in the reflection. Cari had never felt more beautiful than she did that day. Her eyes shone with unshed tears as she saw her lovely daughters, so different but so much the same.

"Mom," Ellie said gently, placing her hand on her mother's arm, "why the tears?"

"I can't believe this is happening! I'm getting married today! A year ago I was facing another year of loneliness, never expecting to find someone to love and share my life with." Tears threatened to spill from her sparkling emerald eyes.

Kate quickly handed her a tissue. "You don't want to smudge your makeup, Mom. It's almost time."

Cari turned to her girls. "Where's Grandpa? I'm ready to start the next chapter in our life."

Kate and Ellie reached out to hold her warm hands in theirs. "Mom, Daddy would be so happy for you and Ray. Honestly, I think it was Dad giving you a push last summer when the tree fell."

Cari pulled her girls in her arms. "You know I love you more than life itself. That will never change."

"Of course we do, forever and always, Mom. Now, what do you say we go and get your last name changed to Davis?" The three McKenna women took one last look in the mirror.

Shane and Dave waited at the bottom of the stairs. Dave flashed back to another day when he walked his girl down an aisle. She was beautiful then but even more so today. She had gone through hard times and appreciated what was good. He reached out and tucked her hand through the crook of his arm—father and daughter, preceded by her children, walked to the French doors of the sunroom.

Cari could see Ray was waiting for her next to their tree. Strains of music wafted softly on the chilly air. Shane pushed the doors open for Kate and Ellie to start the procession. No one paid attention to the temperature. All eyes turned to watch as the family descend the stairs. Shane took his place at his mother's side with his grandfather on the other as they escorted Cari to her future husband.

Ray's eyes caught and held Cari's. She took his strong hand, intertwining their fingers. Any lingering nerves vanished the moment they touched.

The Reverend began to address the small group gathered in the afternoon glow with words of love and commitment. Ray and Cari were lost in each other and the love that surrounded them. Reverend Sussex reached out and covered Ray's and Cari's clasped hands. It was time for their vows. After the wedding rings were placed on the symbolic fingers and the Reverend declared them married, Cari threw her arms around her new husband.

With twinkling eyes, she said, "Mr. Davis, I promise I will love and treasure you for the next thirty-plus years!"

Chuckling, Ray replied, "Mrs. Davis, I promise you we'll fill each day with fun, happiness, and, most of all, love!" Ray kissed his bride.

THE END

23360728R00116

Made in the USA
Middletown, DE
23 August 2015